STEELDUST

Also by J.P.S. Brown

Jim Kane
The Outfit
The Forests of the Night

STEELDUST

J.P.S. Brown

Walker and Company
New York

All the characters and events portrayed in this story are fictitious.

First published in the United States of America in 1986 by the Walker Publishing Company, Inc.

Published simultaneously in Canada by John Wiley & Sons Canada, Limited, Rexdale, Ontario.

Library of Congress Cataloging-in-Publication Data

Brown, J. P. S.
    Steeldust.

    I. Title.
PS3552.R6856S74   1986   813'.54   86-5596
ISBN 0-8027-4065-0

Printed in the United States of America

10 9 8 7 6 5 4 3 2 1

This book is dedicated to the great cattle people who called their horses Steeldust and considered those horses the very best—in a time not long past, but fast-disappearing, when a man who "rode good horses" was usually a good man.

This book is also for folks who ride good horses in these times and for my wife, Patsy, and her mother, Carolyn, and her aunt and uncle, Lou and Gus, the folk who backed the writing of this book.

PREFACE

In early times, even before the Civil War, many Texas cattlemen relocated their stock in other Western states. To
make that journey, they rode a type of horse they called
Steeldust. The original Steel Dust had been one of the fastest
sprinters in the history of Texas and one of the greatest sires
of Texas cowhorses. He was foaled in South Carolina about
the time of the American Revolution and is still recognized
as a foundation sire of the American quarter horse.

Steel Dust's legacy to cattlemen is so great that today,
because they have known his progeny, cattlemen in mountain areas of Mexico who have never heard of the term
quarter horse call that breed the Steeldust horse. Oldtime
ranchers in the West still honor that name, because they
remember his tough prototype, the horse that helped them
make a living after cattle over rocky mountains, through
ponderosa forests, cactus-ridden deserts, and mesquite thickets.

This tale is about one horse who carried Steel Dust's good
name.

CHAPTER 1

A horse is man's old maestro. He carries the manchild, but the child rules. He is the beast of the field, close to the pulse of his Maker.

THE bay mare grazed away from the band without looking back. She stayed in a swale as the band moved away. At moonrise, she stopped in a cedar thicket and began her labor. She gave birth to a stud colt an hour before sunrise.

The colt was sorrel, the color of the sky that spring morning. He took his first steps as a droughty wind came up again that day. He wondered at the eye of his mother and stumbled into her side. She summoned him to her with a soft whiffle. He sought his place, found it, closed his eyes and nursed. He paused once to listen when a lark whistled across the dry flats of his range.

The wind made the bay mare remember her thirst. The country was so dry the band ranged two days away from water to graze its fill. The mare moved her foal out of the cedars and made him travel so she could catch up to the band.

The colt felt great force in his spirit, though his flesh was small. His country was high and cold and laid the snap of the North on his back. Snow lay on the leeward side of the sage and cedar brush and by the loamy hills and ridges.

Springs and tanks were dry. The only water in the country came from windmills on deep wells. The band was moving toward water when the bay mare saw it from the top of a

1

bluff. She called to it. The band stopped and looked up, and the sight of the clean, new foal filled it with emotion. The wind had switched to the mare's favor. The band could not smell the foal, and that gave him great mystery.

The Red Duke, stallion and sire of the band, trotted out, demanding the mare come in and account for herself. The red foal stayed close by his mother as she ambled off the bluff. The stud met her and arched to formally recognize her, standing stock still and touching his nostrils to hers. Then, carefully, respectfully, he inspected the colt and escorted the mare to the band. The other mares acknowledged the red foal, then turned away toward water.

The foal stayed by his mother as he approached the water—he was terrified by the sight of a windmill humming in the wind. The machine of its pumping, the banging of its rods in the earth, the strange symmetry of it, made him press under his mother's side. The band paused often to study the camp surrounding that water. The closer the band drew, the slower it moved, in spite of its thirst.

Wind sprayed water off the brim of a full steel tank by the windmill. A fat stream gushed from a pipe into the tank, which overflowed on a low side with an abundance of clear, cold water.

Two men on horseback rode up and dismounted, unsaddled their horses, left them in a corral, and walked to the tank to drink. They squatted in the sun with their backs against the tank, rolled cigarettes, and watched the mares and colts.

The Red Duke kept watch on the men. The bay mare rushed to the trough to drink. The red foal was stopped by the smell of tobacco and the sound of talk. He located the men. Their hats hid their eyes. He found himself alone, watching the men. The wind shifted and took away their scent. The colt moved in for a better look. One of them straightened a leg toward him and relaxed against the ground. At the same time the wind snatched the man's strong odor back to the colt. The colt wheeled, kicked, shook his head, and trotted away to his mother, disgusted.

The mares drank and rested. Colts lay flat on the sunny ground. The bay mare sauntered to a salt trough, ladled smooth by many big tongues. The colt tasted it and was not interested. He wanted to fly. He stepped away, borne with a lightness that a day of ranging with his mother had not dulled.

"The Duke's thrown another good one," said Tom Ford, the older of the two men.

"He's marked good," said Bill, the other man. "A half moon between his eyes, socks on his hind feet."

"The old stud does credit to your daddy, Bill."

"He marks his colts with steeldust, don't he? Lots of sorrel colts. You know, they say the sorrel is the horse most esteemed by the Arabs. They courted, fought, and did business horseback longer than anybody else, so they ought to know."

"I thought you told me the Arabs liked the brown horse the best."

"I think they believe the dark brown horse is the strongest and most even-tempered, but they say the sorrel treats a man the best."

Tom laughed gently. "I can see plenty about this little feller someone who didn't know he was the best could use against him. He's Roman-nosed. I like him, but his looks wouldn't suit him in a promenade."

"He has a mean ring around his eye, too," said Bill. I like that. It shows the steeldust. He won't have any conceits, but he's wide enough between the ears that he won't let any fool ride him to death."

"He looks like he'll have all a man needs to make a hand," said Tom. "He has the juice he needs and he'll be hard to kill. I bet he'll run as fast as all the rest of the Red Duke's colts too."

"I don't know why I should sit here and worry about him.

This might be the year I quit using horses to make a living. Someday, no more forty-mile circles for me. No more rolling my own cigarettes, nor dry noonings in the cedar shade. Hell, Thomas, this year I might take a vacation, go back to Paris."

"Bill, you could be gone from here five years—like you were for the war—and after five days' cowboying you'd never know you'd been gone, so why do you think you need a vacation?"

"I've decided I'm not going to starve out on this outfit for R.E. Bradford forever. I did it for my daddy, but that was for love. . . . Look at that colt. I bet he was born about yesterday. His mammy has to cover a hundred miles every other day picking to make his milk before she gets back here for a drink and a lick of salt. The way he'll be seeing the country, he should have been born a bird. It occurs to me, I live here, too, make my living the same way he does, almost. I think I'll look around and see if I can get hold of my own outfit.

"Why, Thomas, if I get smart as well as tough, by the time that colt grows to his first saddling, I'll have so much money I'll use thousand-dollar horses to do my ropin' and sortin'. I'll keep a cowpuncher like you to brush them and saddle them, cool 'em down, unsaddle 'em, and put 'em away for me when I'm on the ground. I'll use a roadster to make my circles. In dry times I'll haunt the cool, wet country, and during cold, wet times I'll haunt on down to the sunshiny warm. That way the fine colors of my clothes will never fade and the delicate texture of my skin won't wrinkle. I'll wear alligator boots and a big, white hat like a banker, and when I take off my hat I'll show my hairdo."

"Sounds just right for you. That's success. You won't forget me when you get prosperous, will you, Bill?"

"Not me, Thomas. Say, speaking of prosperous, I've come a long way in poverty and deprivation since breakfast. How about you?"

"You and me headed out at the same time this morning."

"You suppose we can have biscuits and jerky gravy for supper this time?"

"I think so. We have the jerky and flour. Water's exceptional here today, too."

"Right. I'll go fill the buckets."

Bill took their buckets to the windmill and filled them out of a barrel that hung inside the tank under the pipe. Tom Ford made baking-powder dough for biscuits while Bill built a fire in the stove. Then Bill went to the corral and fed hay and grain to the saddle horses. He stayed a moment to watch the Red Duke and his band head for the open country. The Red Duke was an old feller now. He was twenty-six. The mares were keeping flesh on their bones and that was all anyone could expect in a drought. They were what the cowpuncher called "good doers."

The Red Duke had been a two-year-old when Bill was born on the High Lonesome. Bill grew up on the family ranch and joined the Marine Corps in 1917. His parents died in the flu epidemic while Bill was in France, and R.E. Bradford had moved right in and acquired the High Lonesome from the bank.

After being discharged from the service, Bill had gone to Mexico to help a friend gather his cattle. The work had been hard. The man's cattle had been scattered by the revolution. Bill had stayed three years before returning home to Arizona. He had been happy to take a job back on the High Lonesome when R.E. Bradford offered it.

In the hogan, Bill dippered water into a washbasin and washed his face and hands.

"Coffee's on the stove," said Tom. "Don't fill up. You're about to be fed the biscuits and gravy you crave so much."

"Huh, fill up on *your* coffee? How could anybody do that? It probably has a pound of salt in it. Let's see." He tasted it. "Salt in it."

"A pinch of salt in the pot makes good coffee."

"Yeah, but a fistful?"

"It's pleasurable to me."

"Hell, the rest of us didn't camp on an alkali tank when we were learning to drink coffee. Why don't you just put salt in your cup and leave me to flavor my own?"

"It ain't the same. You'll see when you taste somebody else's coffee again."

"Well, you just remember this day when you get the telegram that announces I'm dead. You'll be sorry you fed me so much salt. You'll say, 'Poor Salty Bill, it was me salted him down, ruined his good luck.' "

"Stop your yow-yowing," Tom said. He set a big skillet of jerky gravy and a pan of hot biscuits on the table. "Eat, or you'll never make it to your grave."

The two men ate the gravy and poured molasses on their biscuits for the dessert they called "lick."

"Beans and gravy tomorrow," said Tom, making a cigarette. "I'm looking forward to that."

"When I get to be an international cow buyer, I sure will miss these dinners," said Bill. "The chefs of Paris ain't heard of molasses lick. When I go back, they'll probably give me ice cream with something nasty like a cherry on it."

"You'll probably get off your feed and gaunt up."

"I'll have to worry about my diet, all right. I'll have thousands of cattle to buy while I'm only feeding on steak and seafood, baked potato, and fresh greens with the city fellers. I might never get another decent meal. And they say there's *women* out there."

"Women. Now that is perilous." Tom smiled at his cigarette.

"Blond women, slim. Fleshy dark women. Tiny women with long legs showing through slits in their drawers. Big old fussy-type mamas, too."

"Lordy, Lord, don't think about it."

"My goodness, I'm homesick for this old hogan already. I'm safe here."

Tom was sitting at the table with his tally book and pencil. He sharpened the pencil with his stock knife, looked at the new point, licked it and paused to print with it.

"What's today?" he asked.

"Don't ask me. March 1922?"

"I'll go for that." Tom wrote the date and tallied the birth of the sorrel. "Bay Mare is his dam and Red Duke is his sire." He paused. "Now, give the little feller a name."

"Steeldust," Bill said.

That evening the Red Duke and his mares stopped in a wash in the shelter of cedar-covered breaks. Steeldust felt the first ache of his life in the weariness of his legs. He lay in warm sand and slept.

In the night he awoke to the queer, joyous ravings of coyotes. They tasted at the band's fresh droppings and then, not discouraged, only hungry, went raving on. At dawn, Steeldust was sure he would fly that day. Then Lizard came running by.

Lizard was a red roan colt with black mane and tail, a round, white spot on his forehead, and silver lights on his hide. Bill and Tom called him Lizard because of his skittishness, his quickness, and his habit in repose of letting his tongue hang out as if to see what it might catch while he was resting. He was a rogue for mischief, a genius for dodging the hooves and teeth of the mares. He could show awful fear when a mare chased him to castigate him. But safe again at his mother's side, he would blow out his fear with a snort, shake awhile, wonder at the vehemence of females whose peace he had disrupted, and then move on to new adventures.

When Lizard came by to investigate Steeldust, the bay mare bit him on his round butt so hard he squealed and ran away with his eyes watering. Steeldust followed, began enjoying new freedom with him, and partnered with him from then on.

The spring snow started the grasses. A pair of mountain lions prowled by the band. The Red Duke kept the band in open draws where it could protect itself with senses and speed.

The lions waited. They knew that as more colts were foaled, the mobility and range of the band would be lessened. One still night, the lions started building fear in the band by giving away their scent and sound. The Red Duke roused the band and started it moving. The band had been active and playful in good weather that day. Lizard and Steeldust had been sleeping when the Red Duke made them jump up and run. He did not ask for opinions. He did not put leaving at a run to a vote. He stampeded the band by using as much ferocity as any lion. He put the band under attack, ran it in the open, kept it together and directed its flight.

The band ran until the foals and old mares began to straggle. The Red Duke slowed it awhile, but kept it moving. Finally, he let it stop and rest so the mares and foals could pair up. The foals began to nurse.

One old gray mare began calling for her sorrel filly. The band went on about its business, ignoring her fretting for her foal. She kept looking back and waiting for her colt to answer and come running.

The Red Duke knew the filly had not strayed during the run. She had been lost at the start. The gray mare was old, shiftless, and set in her ways. She had moped about and avoided him when he was trying to arouse the band, looking after herself while she let her filly sleep on the ground. When the Red Duke had caught her, he'd made the hair fly off her, and she did not think of her foal until the other mares began pairing up at the end of the run. Now she would never see her filly again. The Red Duke hazed her into the band and she started grazing, resigned that he would never let her go back for the foal.

The bay mare and the roan mare had made the run

together as partners, loyal to one another even in the panic of flight. They kept track of Steeldust and Lizard and took them close to their sides whenever the pace allowed it. They had no need to call for their offspring when the run was over.

The gray mare's foal was never seen again. The Red Duke knew the lions had chosen his band as prey. He lost another foal a week later. He moved his band to the highest country on the High Lonesome, where deep snow still lay. The band began to lose flesh. The grass had not started in the high country. The band was watering in rock holes where snow melted. It was perishing, while the lions prospered on the new crop of milk-fed colts.

Bill and Tom had begun breaking two-year-old colts. Two weeks passed before they began riding far enough away from camp to realize that the band was being preyed upon.

On the day Bill and Tom began riding their colts for more than an hour at a time, they rode to look for the band. The colts they were riding did not have much range. They were learning to carry weight. The cowboys worked to cure their aimlessness, teaching them they must have no purpose except the purpose of the rider. Each man was riding a string of seven colts. Each man had one older, gentle horse to ride. They crossed the band's tracks miles from its favorite draw. The tracks were deep and showed the band was in distress. Then they found the tracks of the lions.

Bill and Tom lined out for camp and barely spoke to one another until they were at supper.

"Let's take the colts who need the most work and ride until we find the mares," said Tom.

They packed their bedrolls, chuck, and grain on six colts, tied the colts head to tail, and headed out the next morning. Their camp was thirty miles from headquarters. R.E. Bradford had been to the camp with their provision the day before.

He would not return for another ten days. They left him a note: *Gone to find the mares. Lions.*

The band was tiring. The bay mare and the roan were among the few who were not faltering. The lions were always close and bold. They no longer hid. They stayed with the band as though it belonged to them. The band was their camp, their provision.

One evening, Steeldust and Lizard were staying close to their dams because they had been watching the lions all day. The Red Duke was moving them back toward their big draw. He had given up trying to outdistance the lions. His mares were starving. He moved them slowly so he could keep them together.

The lions were playful. They felt no need for caution. They were audacious. They used stealth when they killed, only because they had more fun that way. The big stud and his mares had not opposed them except to run away. They approved of the stud's moving his band to warmer pasture. They did not like the snow either. They wrestled and played as they followed the band, sometimes showing off in full view.

The Red Duke looked up and saw one of the lions lying flat in his path, her tail standing stiff as a fencepost. He hurried to close with the lion. His flared nostrils were red as blood, his sides shrunken and heaving. He was living on heart and nervous drive. He seldom lowered his head to graze. Only his mane and tail retained the gloss and flow of the stallion. His coat was dirty with dried sweat, new sweat, and mud.

At that moment, Steeldust and Lizard saw the second lion behind them. They wheeled to look at him. He lay flat and immobile, staring at them and hiding from the mares. The mares were hurrying after their sire. Their safety lay in staying close to him as he cleared the way. As long as they were moving, they felt protected. They were weary and obedient. Their senses were so full of the lions, they could not think for themselves.

The lion ahead of the Red Duke stood and menaced him. The band panicked and scattered. As Steeldust spun away to catch up to his dam, the lion he had been watching sprang and caught him by the hips. He hooked his claws into Steeldust's rump and hung there to bring him down. Steeldust screamed, and a blood bay fury landed her hooves on the lion's head. The lion rolled away from Steeldust, hugging the ground, his mouth wide and roaring. The bay mare strode over his head again. He scrambled after her and the roan mare wheeled in and kicked him in the jaws with both hind feet. The bay mare dashed over him again and made a jelly of his eye. He hung to her shoulder as she went by, but she jerked free as the roan mare trampled over him with all four feet. The lion wailed with shock. He was such a bully he could not believe he had underestimated the valor of a horse. After all, he only knew the horse's heart was good to eat. He snarled and menaced the mares with his good eye, and the Red Duke fell on his blind side, trapped his striped spine in his jaws and broke his neck. The old stud then danced on the lion's death throes. The other lion, surprised and dismayed that she no longer had power over the band, lined out for her den to hide.

The lioness was conscious her heavy belly was swinging and slowing her down. She was not used to being in this kind of a hurry. Only a few moments ago she had been full of fun and hungry. Now she was afraid. Her meat and play had turned against her, had refused to bow its head.

Bill and Tom topped a ridge on the tracks of the band. They saw the Red Duke and his mares across a draw, then they spotted the lioness. Tom handed his string of colts to Bill, dismounted, and drew his rifle. He sat on the ground behind a cliffrose, braced his elbows with his knees, sighted on the lioness, and waited for her. Bill dismounted.

The lioness came on, her mind distracted by her dismay.

She began climbing the slope toward the ridge where the men were waiting in plain sight. She raised her eyes, saw a man standing beside eight horses waiting for her, watching her from the skyline. A cliffrose by the man was strangely bulky. She could not find the scent on the wind. She veered away from the ridge, took a few steps and stopped for a good look at the men and horses. She felt overwhelmed by horses. Horses were her last sight on earth. Tom's rifle ball killed her instantly.

"Well, I guess we did what we set out to do, so we ought to be proud of ourselves," said Bill as he and Tom sat their horses over the dead lioness. "She was full of kittens, too."

The men took account of the mares who had lost foals. They caught the bay mare and Steeldust and cleaned the lion slashes with antiseptic. The bay mare was gentle and had no fear of the men.

Bill and Tom drove the band back to the big draw. The Red Duke and his mares stayed there and prospered through the growing season. In the first cold days of winter, the men came and weaned the colts off the band. That night the cries of mares and colts kept the cowboys awake.

The men drove the colts away from the windmill a week later. The colts wintered in a pasture by the High Lonesome headquarters. They were fed grain to gentle them and help them grow. Steeldust never saw his mother again. He did not miss her for long, and he did not miss the discipline of the Red Duke. He dearly loved the grain and he loved to romp and range with the other colts in freedom and good health.

CHAPTER 2

His Maker gave the old horse grace and speed, toes, a scrubby mane and tail, and a proboscislike snout that curved toward the ground. Through the centuries, his grace and speed did not allow gripping and clenching, so his feet became his slickest surface. His mane is more like a wing. He hoists his tail like a flag for his spirit. Nothing he does has much to do with the ground. Cast on the ground, he dies.

TWO years after Steeldust was foaled, Bill and Tom began breaking and riding the colts at headquarters. The big draw had been fenced so that the Red Duke's band could not be driven away again by predators. R.E. required that Bill and Tom ride the colts where he could watch them, so he would know when they were hurt.

The stud colts were usually castrated when they were brought in to be ridden. The branding iron and the knife were usually the introductory handshakes the men gave the colts. R.E. decided not to castrate in the spring that year. He was worried about screw worms. The Red Duke was old, and R.E. thought he might also want to keep some studs.

Bill did not mind leaving the colts whole and entirely in possession of all their parts. He intended having his own horse business and he wanted to buy Steeldust and use him as a stud. He didn't tell anyone, but he made up his mind to see a banker as soon as he could get to town.

Bill and Tom ran in the fourteen head of colts that included Lizard and Steeldust and branded them a ℔ on the left jaw. This brand had been designed to resemble a lion's slash and would identify the colts as having been sired by the Red Duke in the year of the lions. The cowboys tied them to black crossties, sacked them out, and began breaking them to lead. The colts were already slaves to barley and oats, so the cowboys used the grain to coax them out of their fear of the training. Once they were over their fear of the men, they only worried the cowboys might not give them all the grain they craved. During the sacking, the men began hanging burlap nosebags on the colts. They began to love the sight of a morral made from a gunnysack because of the grain inside. For the rest of their lives any man could catch them by offering them a morral.

Bill and Tom were watching the colts head out to pasture one evening. The colts were quietly intent on moving far away from the black posts where they had been tied most of the day.

"I like that Steeldust colt," said Bill.

"Aw, he's all right, but he'll never be the horse that Lizard'll be," joked Tom.

"He's already a better horse than Lizard. He has more sense, he's quieter, and he has just as much action. Maybe more. Did you see him kick that sack out of my hand today?"

"You ought not to get so close with that sack. You'll get your head kicked off."

"Where do you suppose he learned to kick like that?"

"I bet he gave his kicking ability a lot of study when that old lion climbed on his rear and took a knife to him."

"His scars sure don't show. He just has ten welts under the hair, one for each lion's claw."

"Well, you better watch him. He'll put welts on your head," said Tom.

"Look at him track. Did you ever see a horse step out straighter than that?"

"Old Lizard has me so spoiled I can't even look at another horse."

"I'm gonna buy him. Me and him are going in the horse business together."

"You couldn't buy a hair on his head. He'd cost you four months' wages, and you and me would be the last people on earth R.E. would sell a horse to."

"I'll own him, all right."

"Yeah? That's a two-hundred-dollar horse. You think R.E. Bradford's going to allow his fifty-dollar-a-month cowboy to own his two-hundred-dollar horse? Hell, no. When that colt's broke, he'll be sold."

"Yeah, and I'll be the one rides him home."

"You're only the feller who'll make him worth two hundred. You won't be able to afford him after you've made a cowhorse out of him. How do you think R.E. would like it if you came riding up on Steeldust someday and he was just what a buyer wanted and you wouldn't sell him? You'd be queering R.E.'s sale. A buyer always wants R.E.'s best horses. He won't take any of the mediocre colts if he can't have first choice of the best ones."

"You're right. My horse wouldn't be for sale. He suits me."

"You're just like everybody else. That's the nature of the horse business: a horseman loses all his sense when he sees a horse he likes. A man might have to own at any cost a horse you and me wouldn't give a nickle for. Makes the world go round, I guess, but if I were you, I wouldn't take too big a shine to Steeldust. He'll be gone before you can raise the price of him."

The cowboys walked toward their quarters. They had bedrooms, a shower with hot running water, an indoor privy, and a woodstove to keep them warm. The headquarters windmill stood right beside their quarters and the cowboys liked the sound of it pumping in the night, working on while they were resting. They liked being comfortable. They were given their meals at R.E.'s table. Mrs. Bradford was good to them. She made their lives gentler. Under her care and feeding they had clean handkerchiefs and napkins every day. They behaved like gentlemen and were turning out gentle colts. Bill and Tom had a wild turn to their hair, but they were decent enough to keep their hair smoothed down around ladies and two-year-old colts.

R.E. Bradford was lying on his lawn chair behind a *tapia,* a wall that surrounded his front yard. The air was so still he could hear every word the cowboys were saying. The cowboys seemed to enjoy headquarters life as long as R.E. did not supervise them. He knew enough to leave them to their work. Once he had offered lengthy advice to Tom on the way he should ride a certain horse. Tom had told him, "Boss, I'm riding this colt and he's too young to ride double. As long as I'm on him you stay off him with your advice."

Now, R.E. watched Bill and Tom work from far away and long ago, meaning he never even let them catch him watching. He envied the pleasure the cowboys took in their work. They laughed and talked so softly he could never hear what they were saying when he wanted most to know. They quieted even more when they became aware of him. Their conversation was invariably about the nature of cattle and horses, whiskey and women. They seldom considered the price of anything. Anything was worthless if it could not be used for cattle, horses, whiskey, and women. They never considered the machinery of business ventures, only the nature of adventures, which was why R.E. knew they would never amount to much.

R.E. had known better than to give Tom advice in the middle of his work. He only offered his help so he could show Tom he knew something about the work and to see if Tom would talk to him. Tom and Bill did not talk to him, that was all, unless the talk was about the nature of a horse or a cow in his business. They only let him know about his products from time to time because he was the one who signed their paychecks. That was all that seemed to concern them, that he keep the business end going so they could go on with their natural lives.

Bill and Tom were also close-mouthed around family men, even those who cowboyed with them. Family men were all "mothered up." Cowboys who married had found themselves another mama. Sooner or later, no matter how tough or able he was, a family man would have to pull up from cowboying and go home to his mama.

R.E. did not know cowboys only held off mothering up as long as nobody wanted them. They only talked big about their disdain for business until a lady came along and put her arms around them and calmed them down and made them be nice. A lot of cowboys joined the society of men on the occasion of being hugged around the neck by a female human.

R.E. had been thinking about doing something nice for his cowboys. He never knew how he stood with them. He knew they liked his stock in horses and that was surely one reason they stayed with him. They liked his stock in whiskey. They drank it readily when he offered it. He decided he kept their loyalty because he did not get familiar with them, so he knew better than to ask them what they wanted as a bonus for their work. He knew he was not much help to them. He would have enjoyed going with them the time they rode the colts after the lions, but he could not cut himself off from the business of the ranch for a day, could not ride a colt for even a hundred yards. Hell, he could not sit in the shade on the same horses Bill and Tom rode all day.

Bill and Tom were sitting in the shade of their quarters waiting for supper. They had washed their faces, combed their hair, and changed their shirts. The colts had come back to water and the cowboys were watching them again. R.E. was still resting behind his *tapia*, out of sight. Steeldust was circling a spot on the ground.

"Hey, the little feller's gonna roll," said Bill.

The colt settled to the ground and lay on his side.

"He's down awful flat," said Tom. "He's probably about to give up the ghost from all the abuse you've been handing him."

The colt rubbed his neck against the ground, rubbed the side of his face, switched his tail in the dust.

"You want to see how a good horse does his toilet? Watch this one roll," said Bill.

The colt sat up and gathered his legs. He snaked his neck along the ground and rolled on his back, kicked and rolled over to his side, stretched his legs along the ground.

"That's one hundred dollars he's worth," said Bill.

The colt rubbed his neck and jaw and the top of his head in the dust. He rolled over again. "That's two hundred," said Bill. The colt rolled again. "That's three."

"If he rolls over again, you won't ever be able to afford him," said Tom. The colt rolled again, stood and shook the dust out of his hide, pointed his nose to the sky, rolled his jaws, and yawned so wide his eyes turned inside out and his tongue flapped out of control. He shut his mouth, gave a tiny start as he became aware the cowboys were watching him. He studied them awhile, and when he saw no morral he turned away to his partners.

"You'll never own that colt if R.E. sees him do that," said Tom. "That yawn made him worth another fifty."

"Ain't he quick about getting his rest? That roll and that yawn wiped out three days' weariness I caused with a railroad tie, a hard twist of rope, and a gunnysack. Now look at him."

Steeldust suddenly decided he was too far away from his fellows. He bucked and kicked and lined out at a dead run to catch up.

"Now, you think he ain't a helluva horse?" asked Bill. "Look how he takes his recreation."

Tom saw R.E. stand up by his lounge. "I bet R.E. saw your horse roll. He'll probably ship him now."

"If he sells that colt, I go too," said Bill. "That's my horse."

R.E. walked to the kitchen door, turned back, and in an even voice said, "Time to eat, fellers. Better come on."

Bill watched him go through the door. Tom was laughing. "Aw, hell," Bill said. "He heard every word I said."

"You just put the man high on his horse, Billy. Tough luck."

The cowboys walked to the main house. Bill was hanging his head. R.E. opened the door for them. Mrs. Bradford smiled, as she always did, when she saw the cowboys coming. Mary, R.E.'s daughter, was smiling by the supper table.

Mary had been away studying at the University of Arizona. She was slim and tan. She wore a light summer dress and sandals. She and her mother always treated Bill and Tom as part of the family. The colts were also part of the family. When Mary was fourteen and fifteen, she had been Bill's tiny partner. Later, she had mooned after him with a fine case of cowboy puppy love. For the past year, though, she had been too sophisticated to hang around her father's cowboys. Now, when she had time for them, she became downright sisterly.

Bill and Tom, their faces burning from the wind and sun of the day, stood solemnly inside the door, taking pleasure in Mary's bare young shoulders and handsome smile while she gave them sisterly hugs. The girl was good stock, and cowboys were always looking for good stock. They regarded R.E.'s daughter as a beautiful person to mate with, not as a sister, or any such kindred within the third degree.

To R.E., Bill and Tom were too wild and rough for his girl. They were the kind of men he would have wanted his sons to be, if he'd had sons, but not the kind he wanted his daughter to marry.

"Look, I did surprise them. They didn't know I was home," said Mary, smiling into Bill's face, holding his hand.

"Tom's blushing," said Mrs. Bradford. She was being familiar with Tom, but careful to keep her distance.

"That's wind and sun," Tom said quietly. "Believe it."

"Let's drink to Mary's homecoming," said R.E. He seldom offered the cowboys a drink in the house. Once in a while he carried a bottle to the corral or the quarters after work. He always gave them a swallow and then carried the bottle back to the house. Now, he handed each cowboy two fingers of bourbon in a large glass. He gave the women each a cocktail and then raised his own glass, an iced amber drink with a mint leaf in it to make him smile.

"To the best crop of two-year-olds I've seen on this ranch," said R.E. Bill and Tom were keeping track of their whiskey portions. Being given whiskey was reason enough for drinking whiskey. They did not need a good crop of colts for an excuse. The ounces disappeared in them like drops of sweat in hell.

At the supper table, Tom entertained the ladies with cowboy stories. Bill paid for his supper by being still. These were good people he was working for, and the blue-eyed, black-haired girl seemed to enjoy looking him in the eye. Bill liked those blue eyes gazing happily and unselfishly at him all through his supper. He liked the way she moved now that she was grown. He decided he finally must be dissipating. He was actually looking into the eyes of the boss's daughter on the same day he decided to own one of the boss's horses. With all that on his mind, Bill was smart enough to keep his mouth shut. He ate his supper and left as soon as he could.

The next morning Bill went out to wrangle the colts for their first saddling. He rode in behind Steeldust and watched the way he walked. The colt's legs formed a broad V from his muscular shoulders and hips to his toes as they stepped out straight ahead. Bill's pleasures were simple. He enjoyed watching one horse more than all others. He could see that Steeldust harbored great power and carried it with great poise. He would never be anyone's pet. He had been caught by a lion and had shed the beast. Some oldtimers believed a colt that had been caught by a lion would never be a saddle horse, would never stand still to be held and saddled, ridden and worked.

Bill believed all colts had to be noble to go through life so naked. They had no armor and no weapon but their spirit. They had no claws, no fangs, and were free of all adornments except their own hair and eyes. They had no camouflage. They could not deceive. The colt would be with men now for the rest of his life, whether they whipped him, petted him, pitied him, or respected him, and Bill had the responsibility of showing him the way. Some of the colts would become race horses and run until the track and the hauling broke them down. Most would become cowhorses. Fifty different men might own them before their lives ended.

Some men would use these horses to go on parade, adorning themselves and the horses with a weight of outlandish clothing and silver paraphernalia to enhance the picture they made. These men proclaimed, "I boss a fine horse, so don't look at the horse, look at me."

This was the last morning these colts would move with the abandon they enjoyed now. Their backs would be sore when they went out to pasture again this evening after they had carried the weight of man and entered his service. No colt was ever as clean and whole again, his step never as spry and happy, his hide never as loose, as now, this last time he was wrangled before his first saddling.

Colts that were trained by the wrong men were not able to keep their poise under the weight of a man. Excited men made excited horses who squirmed under the saddle all their lives. They threw their heads, ground their teeth, pranced high and danced sideways to recover the liberty they were feeling now, for the last time.

Steeldust was not so surprised at being saddled. He had been saddled many times when Bill was sacking him out. He was surprised when he began to carry Bill's weight. Each new sound and movement of the man and saddle startled him. The world looked different to him with a man on his back, but he never offered to buck. Bill did not manhandle him. He did not try to teach him lessons he must learn for himself in his first saddling. Bill only wanted him to step out and travel while he introduced him to the hackamore rein.

Steeldust traveled for an hour. He stubbed his toes on the turpentine weed, stumbled through cactus, thrashed over the sagebrush. He fell into washes with Bill's weight bearing down on him and then had to pack Bill out of them. He had to learn to watch where he was going instead of watching Bill. He could not help being startled when a dove flew under his hoof, or when Bill coughed or struck a match, but he did not feel abused or afraid his world had come to an end when Bill reined him in at the corral and dismounted. Bill unsaddled him, rubbed him, scratched his ears and gave him grain in his morral. Steeldust closed his eyes and fed on the grain and forgot his first saddling.

After a month, Steeldust was considered to be "rough broke." He was following Bill around the corral begging for grain. Under Bill's rein, he was looking at cattle and turning them back. He seemed to enjoy the touch of Bill's hand. He was growing and strengthening. He often seemed to learn his lesson before Bill had time to finish teaching it to him. Bill began to give him extra time. Steeldust kept him in a good humor. His most used expression around colts was "Come on, little feller, come on," and Steeldust always came on without reservation.

By the time Steeldust was a three-year-old, he was the top colt in Bill's string of saddle horses. Bill was a good judge of horses, and he was objective about colts he rode and trained for other men, but he felt privileged to ride Steeldust. He did his best for every colt he rode, but as happens to all horsemen who know some good horses in their lives, he had finally fallen into a passion for one horse.

One day, Pete Kapp, the cow buyer, came to the ranch to do business. Bill rode Steeldust and Tom rode Lizard to drive in a bunch of heifers Kapp had come to buy. Kapp leaned against his dusty touring car, smoked a cigar, and watched Lizard and Steeldust at work.

Bill and Tom let their colts stay back to keep from crowding the heifers at the gate. The cowboys looked neither to the right nor to the left. They had been unfriendly with Kapp for years and they called no greeting to him. He had no regard at all for them. He was watching Lizard and Steeldust. He knew the cowboys would not ride colts they did not respect and trust on a day the ranch was shipping cattle.

A heifer in the drag shied at a gatepost, skittered along the fence, threw her tail up, and dashed for the faraway. Lizard, eyes glinting, slid into the ground ahead of her, blocked her way, turned with her, and headed her back through the gate. He stood quietly as Tom dismounted and closed the gate behind the cattle.

Bill unsaddled Steeldust, turned him out, and slapped him on the rump so he would run off, out of sight. He trotted a step, yawned, looked back, lolled his tongue at Bill, nodded, then ambled out of Bill's reach to wait for Lizard. Bill saddled another horse as he listened to R.E. brag to Kapp on the way Lizard worked cattle.

Bill drove the heifers into an alley where Tom could cut out the cattle Kapp did not want. He stopped his horse in a gate to work the alley, and R.E. walked up to his stirrup. Bill could tell by the way R.E. was looking at him that he was about to betray them all.

"Why'd you turn the other colt out?" asked R.E., grinning at Bill.

"He's too green for these salty heifers."

"You'll only be cutting in the alley. Kapp wants to see him work. He might buy him."

"I wish I'd known he wanted him."

"You don't mind if I catch him, do you?"

"He belongs to you."

Bill watched R.E. out of the corner of his eye as he walked to Steeldust with a morral. Steeldust came to him in a hurry.

Anytime he saw a morral, he fell into a craving and did not care who was carrying it. R.E. let him have a few bites and then haltered him. He turned and grinned at Bill.

Bill put his saddle on Steeldust again, and he and Tom cut the cattle. Bill could have made Steeldust look bad, but he did not have that kind of treachery in him. To make the colt do wrong would have confused him and would not have been consistent with the trust that was growing between the man and the horse about the right way to work cattle. To turn him away from cattle when he had been taught to turn with them would have been a betrayal the colt would instantly feel.

Bill unsaddled Steeldust at noon, realizing he might never ride him again. R.E. called Bill and Tom to his office and poured coffee for them. Pete Kapp left the ranch, a sign he had pulled off some cow buyer's trick and did not want to have to look anybody in the eye. R.E. sat at his desk with a guilty look on his face.

"Fellers," said R.E., "those colts you rode are the best-trained young horses I've ever seen. I'm grateful to you once more."

"The one I'm riding still needs work," said Bill, looking into the bottom of a dark corner of the room.

"Pete Kapp wants to buy both colts. He'd rather have the colts than the heifers."

"How much are you asking for the colt I've been riding, if you don't mind telling me?" asked Bill.

"How much do you think he's worth, Bill?"

"I'd be awful high on him."

"How high? You broke him. I need your opinion."

"He's valuable, all right."

"Let me put it this way. How much would you give for him?"

"I'd give you six months' wages. In fact, if I have any credit with you, I'll buy the colt right now."

"Kapp offered me the cash it would take you a year to earn cowboying."

"I can't match that. My whole outfit'll be worn out in six months. I can't go naked just so I can own a horse."

"I have to sell all the colts. This horse business has been operating at a loss too long. I'm keeping a remuda of forty or fifty saddle horses and everything else is for sale. I'm selling the mares, too."

Bill and Tom looked at each other and laughed. "There goes my horse," said Bill.

"Oh, *si*," said Tom.

"We have to move the cattle to the desert, where it can make a living while this ranch recuperates from the drought," said R.E. "We have to go to browse this winter and spring and give the High Lonesome grass a chance to come back."

"I'd be leaving when the red colt was gone anyway," said Bill. "So I guess I won't have to quit. I'll go with the herd. What'll you do with the Red Duke?"

"We'll retire him and leave him here the rest of his days," said R.E. "Which brings me down to facts. I've been trying to find a way of expressing my appreciation for you two. I've decided to give you each six months' wages or the colt of your choice. I'd give you a year's wages, but I need money to hold this outfit together. I'm giving you this because I might not be able to keep you full-time after we bring the herd back from Red Rock. I'd better give it to you now. I might not have it to give in six or eight months.

"For years I believed everything I owned had to be for sale, if I was to stay in business. You taught me that anyone who says everything he has is for sale is more interested in selling out than he is in standing fast and raising good livestock and keeping good help. I have too many good horses, thanks to you two. I want to see you both well mounted before I sell them all. You deserve the best this outfit has raised and trained. If you take the money, it will be the last I'll ever give for green horses, mares, studs, or horsebreakers and you're welcome to it."

The office was quiet awhile.

"I'd like to own the sorrel colt," Bill finally said.

"Fine," said R.E. "How about you, Tom?"

"If you can get a year of my wages for Lizard, he'd better be sold," said Tom. "You need him more than I do. I'll take six months' wages and thank you. I already have a top horse who needs all the work I can give him, or he'll start bucking me off."

Bill and Tom bathed and changed, climbed into the backseat of the company roadster and headed for town with R.E. and his family. Bill watched Mary joke with her folks in the front seat on the way to town. She made them laugh, and Bill caught himself smiling, even though she was not including him and Tom in her fun. She was no baby, however. She was not acting the sophisticated lady now, but she kept a reserve about her that showed she could make any day go by in a manner that pretty much suited her. She was like a year-and-a-half-old filly who was still running with her dam. She could wean herself away any time she saw fit, and never look back. She reminded Bill of Natalia, his mother.

Bill had kept a family picture, a painting. The artist had made the picture when Bill was an infant. Natalia was sitting her horse sidesaddle, holding Bill on her hip. Bill's father was facing her on his top horse, Baldy. Between them was a snaky old cow, head up, and looking far away under ear-marked ears. Her feet were barely touching the ground. She was big-horned and salty, looking to escape and not knowing which way to go. Bill's father was trying to cut the cow out of a herd and Natalia was mischievously turning her back toward the herd. Sam, the horse Natalia was riding, was spinning with the cow, head down, intent. Natalia was laughing. William Henry Shane, Sr. looked stern. Baldy's head was up and he had one ear on his rider and one on Natalia. He had decided he would have to figure out the people before he could ever know what to do about the cow. Bill was grinning with his tongue out and watching the cow so she would not get away.

The first eighteen years of Bill's life had been full of that kind of fun. Then he felt restless and joined the Marines. His folks went to Phoenix, caught the flu, and died. Bill still felt guilty about leaving them. Now he had decided it was time he took hold of his father's dream. His father had said, "Billy, I went a long way toward being the kind of man I wanted to be when I was able to make up my mind about a few principles. I decided early on I needed to own but a few head of hardy livestock and a good place to keep them and your mother happy. When a man finally decides on one horse, one woman, one God, and one country, he can go on and live a good life. Until he does that, he ain't worth killing." Bill knew God and he had shown he could serve his country. He might not be sparking one woman, yet, but he was ready for the horse and he knew which one he wanted.

This was the day Bill was going to a banker with the project his father had passed on to him. This banker, Richard Claire, was not the one who had handled his father's account, but he had been there to settle it after Bill's father died.

Bill decided this banker might be a good man, even if he did look like a salamander. He must be willing to back cattlemen and horsemen; he kept plenty of reminders of the good that cattle and horses had done his bank. Walls and other spaces were adorned with the heads of great horned steers and paintings and sculptures of cattlemen and horsemen doing their business.

Claire's secretary escorted Bill to the door and the banker ushered him to a seat in his office. Bill sat across the desk and listened to the man talk important business with his secretary for a while. In spite of himself, Bill was more critical of the way the man looked every time he saw him. This time, the man's gray hair was blue. Every time Bill saw him, his hair was a different color. The man's cap of hair was so neatly arranged that Bill figured someone must have taken an indecent amount of time doing it. The man must be real careful about touching his own head. Bill just could not understand how such a hairdo could materialize so perfectly to adorn a working man's head, whether he started his day shuffling paper and estimating another man's worth or roping a bronc to saddle in the dark.

Bill knew he was probably wrong to breathe in that the man was false and then breathe out with a plea for a loan. He tried to get over being snobbish about the way the man looked. The man was dressed in exceptionally fine clothes, which went with being a banker. A high polish on shoe and fingernail went with being a banker too. Bill supposed he did that to his nails himself. Where in the world could he have it done?

Claire produced a smooth, flat cigarette case, offered Bill a tailor-made smoke, and lit one himself. From the same case he detached a fine golden piece of cutlery for the trimming of his nails. He made conversation about R.E., how fine a girl Mary was, how fine a cook Miz Bradford was, and about the weather. He showed exceptional knowledge of the dryness of the year and its effect on the livestock while he was paring his nails.

Finally he asked, "What brings you to us, Bill? I've been wondering when you'd make it in here to do some business."

"I've been holding off doing any business, but I want to start now," Bill said.

"Fine. That's the kind of talk I like to hear. But now, uh, before we go further, I, uh, would like to stress one point. You're a man of many talents, I'm sure, so there's a lotta ways we can do business, but, uh, I can only give you an unequivocal no if you've come to us for a loan involving land or livestock. Also, we will require extraordinary collateral before we extend any kind of business loan.

"On the other hand, you, my friend, can, uh, qualify for a small loan with nothing but your signature. We'll be happy to have you in the family. We, uh, are prepared to loan you as much as, uh, fifty dollars. Pay it back whenever you like. I never saw a cowboy who wasn't short of money when he came to town."

Bill knew he was on the wrong train, but rather than be impolite, and figuring he could hurt himself by pointing out to the man that he was a fake and a salamander after all, Bill pressed on.

"Sure, I didn't think you'd loan me money without collateral, but I didn't think you had me figured as a man who needed fifty bucks to start a shoeshine business, either," said Bill. "If you'll just sit still a minute, I'd like to talk business and find out just how dead set you really are against making me a loan."

"I, uh . . . all right," said Claire. He looked in Bill's face to see if Bill could make him do anything he did not want to do, decided he could not, looked at his watch, snapped shut its cover, and put it back in his vest pocket. He folded his manicured hands in front of him, where he could look at them while he had to listen to Bill. He glanced out the door to see if he could catch his secretary's eye. "Please be brief," he said.

"Down in Red Rock, where R.E. winters his cattle, he's been using a ranch that belongs to me. The land is twenty sections of deeded and ten sections of state grazing lease. I've been paying the taxes and the lease on that land since 1917. It borders the bigger ranch that R.E. now owns. My land was never fenced separately and R.E. has been using it as if he owns it.

"Before my folks gave me that land, my dad drilled six wells on it. He dug canals for irrigation and leveled three hundred acres. I can put up that land and the wells for collateral on a loan. R.E.'s been welcome to use everything there up to now, but now I want to grow feed, start a herd of cattle of my own, and raise good horses. R.E. just gave me my pick of his stud colts and I want to buy back all those HL mares.''

Claire had been listening so attentively he forgot about his manicure. "You say you own twenty sections of R.E.'s ranch at Red Rock?" he asked.

"R.E. bought all my dad's land and probably thinks he owns mine, too. I haven't said anything to him about it, because I didn't mind him using it, but ten percent of the two hundred sections he bought from the bank belongs to me."

"Oh my, I'm afraid you're very much mistaken. Those wells can't be on your property. The bank took over all your father's property right after he died. Your being away in France at that time explains your ignorance and that . . . that . . . I'm sorry to disappoint you, but that ranch doesn't belong to you at all. The bank sold it to R.E. Bradford.''

"You better look at my copy of the survey and deed. Those twenty sections have been mine since before I shipped to France.''

Bill took the documents for his land out of his hip pocket, unfolded them, and spread them in front of the banker. Claire scanned them and pushed them back. Right then Bill decided Claire had a personal interest in his land and was trying to hide it. Any banker could see at a glance that the papers were the right kind to back Bill's claim. It occurred to Bill that Claire must have known about them.

"How about it?" Bill asked. "Will you consider the loan?"

Claire leaned back in his chair. "Well, I, uh . . . just like I told you before, we're . . . we're . . . this bank isn't . . . would not be able to even consider on . . . on that . . . anything of that sort. Uh, we, uh, deal with cattlemen, first of all, not farmers. Then again, right now, we're not even really dealing much with cattlemen. We . . . we're not giving out cattle loans, except to our established customers. Cattle are cheap in a drought, you understand. Doesn't look like it's gonna get better very soon, either. And *horses* . . . you talk about puttin' out *horses* . . . buyin' those horses of R.E.'s . . . off that range. Why, those mares aren't worth a nickle. Why, R.E. . . . R.E. . . . The best thing he can do is get rid of those mares—if he can possibly do it. The best thing by far to do is not own any . . . as quickly . . . no matter how much it costs him. He oughta get rid of those mares. Horses? They're not worth . . . not worth killin'."

"Look here," said Bill, "I didn't come in here for that kind of talk. It seems to me people need good horses in the livestock business, especially when the country's doing bad. I'd think bringing that Steeldust blood here was one of the best favors my dad ever did."

"Well, not to say anything bad about your daddy's business sense, him being dead and all—and your mother—but your daddy didn't always do right. When he came to this country, he . . . went kinda wild . . . and he . . . the proof of that was . . . when he died he was so deeply in debt to us we had to take his property. After we settled our claim with his lawyers, your daddy's property was all gone—and we wrote off a lot more on his account than his property was able to pay. You know, your daddy and mother, they . . . they weren't very good business people. They . . . they, uh, did as they pleased too much. They, uh, happened to have a banker at that time, my predecessor, who was broad-minded and who would go with them on their wild schemes, but he retired about the time your daddy died, and things got a little bit tough until I took over the account. It's probably a good thing your daddy and mother died when they did, because, uh, they—they were . . . plumb out of credit."

Wrath had begun to take hold of Bill before the banker had been able to get this last sentence out of his mouth. "A good thing?" he asked. "A good thing they died because they were out of credit with the likes of you? Why, you son of a bitch, I don't think it was such a good thing. Good thing for you bankers, maybe. You got to keep everything they'd worked for. Good thing for a son of a bitch like you. If they hadn't died when they did, you'd probably still be a cashier. You'd better get right with me before I get out of this chair, or I'm going to strangle you with your spotted necktie."

"Wooooooo . . . whoooooooaaaaaaah, don't get me wrong, now! Don't get me wrong . . . Maybe that didn't sound just right, but I'm just talkin' like a good businessman. Don't get me wrong—I'm sorry they died—I sympathize with you altogether . . . you know, both of them dying like that in their prime, but your daddy didn't do everything just right. He, you know, and then he and your mother liked to have fun. They went on all those trips, had everything they wanted, saw the cities . . . uh, gambling, too . . . Your daddy got into this bank awful deep. We had a lot of cleaning up to do . . . uh . . . when he . . . died. If I'd been handling his account, things would have been a lot different."

"This bank was different before you took over, that's the damned truth. It's a good thing I came in here after all."

"Why's that, uh, Shane?"

"I've been long overdue coming in here and finding out what you've probably been thinking and saying about my folks. It's time I made you take it back."

"Well, I'm awfully sorry, uh, you can be sure. I sure am. It was an unfortunate choice of words."

Bill stood up, and Claire opened his eyes wider to see him better. "I apologize, now. I sure do," he said.

"Remember this, salamander. Water dog. My folks had more style in the way they turned their heads to look away from you than you'll ever see if you live to turn the keys to a hundred of these banks."

"That they did. They did have style. Good people, that's right, good people."

Bill turned to leave. Claire laid back in his chair. "Let me say this," he said. "There's never been a more authentic westerner or more honest-to-goodness cowman anywhere than your father. You look like you fit the role too. You're the authentic article, all right."

"Yeah? You are too," Bill said, and walked out.

Claire let Bill leave the building and then called in his secretary. "Uh, Margaret, make notes here. First of all, find out if R.E. Bradford's in town. I want to talk to him. Then, check at the county seat down in, uh, Pima County and find out if any of that Red Rock country of R.E.'s belongs to Bill Shane. Find out about that for sure. Then, get hold of the county agent down there and find out how deep those wells are and how much water can be pumped out of that ground and how fast."

CHAPTER 3

All the world knows the horse is good, and a certain kind of man believes that if he keeps a horse he can show how good he is. That man is fooling himself if he believes his horse loves him. That man's horse loves only the matchless horse.

PETE Kapp came back that summer with trucks and bought all the High Lonesome colts. Steeldust stood in a pasture by himself and watched as Lizard and his brothers were driven away. The colts kept trying to turn back. Lizard broke away and pranced out into the flat with his tail up in a plume, until two cowboys rode out after him and led him back to the bunch with his head down. Dust rose behind the colts and Steeldust nickered to them as they went out of sight.

Bill went out to talk to Steeldust and give him sympathy. He called him into the corral and hung a morral on him. The absence of Lizard did not hurt the colt's appetite, and this was a consolation to Bill. Bill could forget about Lizard if Steeldust could. He walked away to clean up for supper. He knew he would not be lonesome for Lizard when he was in the company of Miss Mary and a drink of R.E.'s whiskey. Nature gave him that easy remedy for missing a horse. He had not found as simple a remedy for being lonesome for people.

A crew was being hired for the drive to the desert. Neighbors were arriving and adding their cattle to the High Lonesome herd. The desert would provide browse and warmth for the herd through the winter and spring. If it rained that winter, cattle would graze on lush filaree and Indian wheat on a desert that extended from just below the Mogollon Rim in Arizona all the way to the Sea of Cortez in Mexico.

People were arriving on horseback, in wagons and motor cars. Mary had invited her friends to a swimming party in the steel tank under the windmill. Families were pitching tents and cowboys were stretching rope corrals in a cottonwood grove in the big draw below headquarters. Cooking fires were burning. The cattle were being turned loose in the draw until the drive began.

This reunion gave the men a chance to show off their horses and cattle and the women to cook and visit and show off their children. After a day and a night of play, the crew would begin the roundup of R.E.'s cattle.

Mary's friends were arriving and she was hurrying about to greet them. After noon, Bill went to the corral to shoe Steeldust.

Steeldust was hard to shoe, but he did not mind being shod. He just leaned on Bill and dozed while Bill's back propped him up. Bill's bones and thighs creaked under the weight while he did the horse the big favor he would have to do him all his life.

The August afternoon was hot and Bill could see thunderheads to the south a hundred miles away. He was sure they would lay their moisture somewhere else and not on the High Lonesome. He finished shoeing Steeldust's front feet and he stood away and straightened his back. He heard a shout of pleasure from the stock tank and he saw a tanned body hurtle off the windmill tower into the water. The abundant water splashed, washed, and sprayed. Smiling heads and inner tubes bobbed above the rim of the tank.

Bill liked watching Mary and her friends the way he enjoyed a drink of water when he and Tom had been riding all day. Once in a while, Bill and Tom swam in a windmill tank, or in a full dirt tank in a draw on their way home after their work was done. They never swam in the tank at head-quarters, where R.E.'s family could see them. They had enough trouble when their horses saw them. They were always careful to tie their horses securely to a tree a good distance from the place where they swam. The sight of the cowboys' hatless, naked carcasses—suddenly showing against their burnt faces, necks, hands and wrists—scared cow horses out of their wits.

Bill was finishing his shoeing when Mary came into the corral to stand and watch him. Her hair was wet against her head, her face washed bare from the swim, water still lying in her brows. Her worries were gone. She was a long-legged, tanned, smart, sound young lady, and Bill was discovering an awful passion for her.

Steeldust revived when Mary came near. He blew against her breast and began investigating her. He raised his head and whiffed at her neck and ear and began to nibble there, smelling her lilacs. He was sniffing a lot closer to the lilacs than seemed decent to Bill. He led a damned privileged life, freely availing himself of the pleasures of nuzzle and smell any time he felt like it. He made Bill feel downright neglected.

Mary began petting Steeldust's big neck and hugging his jaw against her cheek. He went away into a stupor, fondled into a state of shock. He collapsed against Bill and paid no more attention to him than he would to a corner post. Bill finished shoeing him, then saddled him and led him away from Mary. "Don't be pettin' my horse, Mary," he said.

"Are you going after the remuda now?" asked Mary.

"Yes."

"My friends want to go riding."

"Your daddy doesn't raise good horses for your friends to joy-ride. You don't want to get 'em bucked off, do you?"

"They're all good riders."

"I thought you knew the difference between people who could ride and those children who just climbed out of a swimming party with their round little butts all wrinkled from the soaking.''

Mary's eyes glittered with temper. "Bill, right this minute, riding's just a way for me and my friends to have fun. Don't give me cowboy rules, just please wrangle the horses.''

Bill stepped on his horse and rode away. Mary had been spending too much time in town. She was in too big a hurry to have fun. For the past year or two, she had seldom been at the ranch. In the summer, she came and "tried horseback riding" with her friends. The circles they rode were short so Mary could have them back on the patio in time for lemonade and a sit in the shade before they got thirsty. She never did any work. She never made a hand. She looked on cowboy work as child's play and seemed to think only children wanted to be cowboys. Grown people only cowboyed while they were waiting for something better to do. Mary's schooling was taking her away from the ranch in the worst kind of way, making a city girl out of a cowgirl.

Steeldust was ambling along as though Mary had stroked him into a desire for early hibernation. Exasperated, Bill spurred him hard to wake him up and he snorted out the lilacs, quaked three feet off the ground, and bucked straight off a steep hill. Bill sat up straight, grinned, and rode him. The horse threw up his head and quit about the same time Bill ran out of wind at the bottom of the hill. Bill looked back to see if anyone had seen him make the ride. He saw not a soul. He was as sure as wind blew in a drought that Steeldust would have piled him on his head if Mary had been watching.

Bill and Steeldust went on with the work at hand. They crossed the ridges with the new iron shoes, found the remuda, and drove it in.

The horses ran headlong for the gate the last quarter mile to the corrals. They braked and skidded, dodged the gateposts, and slammed into the corral in a bunch. They whirled with their heads high and arrogant, nickering at the cedar ridges they had left behind, snorting at Mary's friends on the corral fence.

Bill could see more wagons and roadsters of visitors converging on the cottonwood grove as he walked Steeldust to the corral. He dismounted to close the gate. None of the city kids on the fence said hello. All dudes loved to sit on a fence when cowboys were trying to work in a pen. A dude on a fence was in the way, a distraction to the livestock. Mary knew this, but she had climbed the fence just like all the rest of the dudes. She was bragging on Steeldust to her boyfriend, Tony Claire. Tony was Mary's age, son of Claire the banker. Bill did not like him and did not like people coveting his horse while they ignored him and sat on the fence in the way. He knew he was carrying an awful chip on his shoulder only because he had been sweating while Mary and her boyfriend were in swimming. He had made a bronc ride and Mary had not seen it. Now she had lined up a gallery to watch him work and he would probably do something awkward.

Dudes certainly did not bother Steeldust and make him cranky. Mary and her girlfriends came off the fence to pet him. Mary hugged his face to show the girls how he whiffed at her sweetest-scented places. Then, with the petting, he went moribund.

"Why are you looking at me like that?" Mary asked Bill.

"He'll chew off your ear someday. He'll think it's a daisy. You'll have to comb your hair longer on that side." Bill laughed as though he had said something funny.

"Are you kidding? He's too much of a dear to bite anybody." Mary was gazing at Bill's horse as though he was just her very own handsome pet.

Tony moved off the fence to stand in the saddlehouse door, where he could be more in the way. He did not step aside when Bill started through. He probably did not want to fight Bill. He just did not have sense enough to stand out of a door when a man needed to pass through to do his work.

Bill stood back and waited. Claire, Tony's father, was also standing by the door.

"I understand we're to be business associates after all," said Claire. Bill turned to see if Mary was watching before he spoke to Claire. She was petting Steeldust under the chin with the tips of her fingers and staring at Bill and waiting to see what his answer would be. Debris from a tiny wind swirled at Bill's feet, then grew taller and made Claire's suit billow with dust. Bill knew bankers seldom found themselves caught out in the wind, but this one was holding down his hat in the dust so he could be by the side of his overgrown son.

Tony was carrying a .45-caliber pistol for his visit to the country. People from town enjoyed bringing their dogs and guns to ranches with the notion that dogs and guns were free in the country. The moving targets their bullets could find were free and the animals the dogs chased, terrorized, and killed were free for the killing. Being hospitable, ranchers usually did not prohibit a city man from bringing his dog and gun for a visit, but they always worried about the animals under their charge a gun might kill. A rancher did not like it when someone's town dog was unloaded in his yard to make a beeline for his chickens, fight with his cow dogs, and chase his livestock. People from town did not mind inconveniencing the rancher for their dogs' sake, though.

Claire laid his arm over Tony's shoulder and grinned at Bill.

"Which one is the horse old R.E. gave you to start your herd?" asked Tony. "If it's the one Mary's petting, he don't look much like a herd sire to me."

"What do you know about a horse?" said Bill. "I could talk about horses, and before three minutes were up you'd ask your daddy for a Baby Ruth."

Steeldust was standing with his head over Mary's shoulder, chewing grain out of the palm of her hand, resting his chin against her breast, his eyes vacant as an idiot's. He lolled his tongue and opened his mouth wide to dislodge grain from his back teeth. He was immune to Bill's dirty looks.

"Where have you been, Shane?" Claire asked. "I bought all R.E.'s colts. Yours is the only one I didn't get."

"I thought Kapp bought those horses."

"Yes, he did it with my checkbook."

"What use would you have for a good horse?"

"Kapp, R.E., and I will be partnering feeding cattle on the desert. I have a big interest in these High Lonesome cattle now. We need good horses. Tony just came up from the desert at Red Rock. He can tell you about the kind of work and training our colts will need."

"How come you're keeping this colt for a stud?" asked Tony. "We're emasculating them all. Not a one of them is fine enough to make a stallion."

"This one's a stud because he suits me," said Bill.

"He'll make a fine horse, no doubt," said Claire. "I'd have to reserve my opinion until he's grown and, uh, I see who does his training, though." He backed into the saddlehouse so the wind would not bother his composure again. "However, I'll buy him just so I can say I bought 'em all. How much do you want for him?"

Bill did not answer.

"I'll give you two hundred dollars cash for him," said Tony.

Bill laughed. "You? You'd be wasting your money. You couldn't get two hundred dollars' use out of any horse alive."

"Does that mean you're turning it down?" asked Tony.

"Yessir."

"By damn, two fools just met and I was the witness," said Claire. "Tony is a fool for offering too much for a horse and Shane is another for turning it down."

Claire and Tony followed Bill around the corral as he caught horses.

"Have you hired your crew for the drive yet, Shane?" asked Claire.

"That's the reason for all the damned society bunching up here, ain't it?" asked Bill. "So we can hire a crew and make a drive?"

"I guess you'll be hiring mostly Indians and Mexicans, as usual. Why not hire Tony? He's an athlete and well educated. Pay him a little more and you can have him."

"We probably can't afford him. He'd be too high-powered to cowboy with this outfit."

"Hell, you and I are business associates now. You ought to hire my son."

"I'll tell you what to do. Put him on your payroll and furnish him a string of horses to ride, get R.E. to guarantee he won't be in the way, and I'll let him come along."

"Ah, hahaaa, good," said Claire.

Mary was still fondling the horse and looking down her nose at Bill. She knew it griped him that she and his horse were breaking his rules. She knew he never petted his horses. He did not like being patted and stroked by the man who put him to work, either. He put his head down and saddled the horses for Mary's friends and did not look up until they had all ridden away.

Bill and Tom spent the afternoon bringing in a barren cow they had been saving to butcher for the reunion. Tom roped her in the pasture and gave her slack while Bill hazed her to the cottonwoods. They ran her through wagons and tents and the crowd of visitors and tied her to a tree and left her to cool off.

Bill gave Steeldust a drink in the shade and dismounted. He looked up and saw a new Ford truck heading fast toward him. A calf was sleeping in the sun with his head turned back along his side close to the edge of the road. The driver veered the truck toward the calf as he passed him, barely missing him. The truck skidded to a stop under the trees by Bill. The driver was Tony Claire. His father was riding with him in the front seat. The back of the truck was loaded with more of Mary's young friends from town. They were all laughing when they jumped down from the truck. Tony looked back to see if he had missed the calf. The calf was running to his mother.

"Cute," Bill said. "If the little feller had raised his head, you would have hit him."

"I missed him, though, didn't I?" Tony said, laughing.

A horseman hailed the group, ran in, jerked his horse's head skyward, and slid him to a stop. He was Mahout Lindano, Claire's foreman. He shook Tony's hand from atop his horse. Lindano was the Mexican trade name for a strong cattle dip used by ranchers for eliminating lice and ticks. Lindano was also this short, squat man. His face always carried a Neanderthal grimace, with beetling brows, flat nose, wide mouth, and gapped teeth. His mustache and the hair on his head bristled unevenly away from his skull. It stood apart from his head as though electricity was working there and he was on a stampede from Saint Elmo's fire. He wore a big sombrero with the brim turned down in front and back, which made him look like he was hiding under a rock. His nature was to whip all animals and men in his charge who would stand near enough to take it. He used chains for whipping his animals. He cheated his help of their wages and gambled away the money on horses he whipped. Horseflesh was his obsession. Bill believed he would murder for a horse he coveted, and his cruelty to horses had mounted a large account he someday would have to settle with Bill. That account was one—another was his penchant for stealing cattle.

Bill had first met Lindano three years before, when R.E. hired him for the drive to the desert. During the drive, he had come to Bill with a long story about how he had lost twenty big steers. Bill went on with the drive but sent Lindano back for the cattle and kept him on the payroll. A month later Lindano came to the winter headquarters at

Red Rock for his paycheck, but he still had not found the cattle. Bill paid him, fired him, and never recovered the stock.

Later, Bill met the constable from the region where the cattle had been lost. The constable told Bill that Lindano had never come back to look for any lost cattle.

Now Lindano was sitting his horse, his mouth grinning like a jack-o'-lantern. Tony had hooked his thumbs into the belt of his short-sleeved safari jacket and was squared off in front of Bill as though pleased with himself for having been born a rich kid.

"You've met my father's new foreman, Mahout Lindano, I suppose," Tony said to Bill. "He'll be representing our interests on the drive, you see."

"Never heard of him," said Bill. Lindano laughed and moved his horse for a better look at Steeldust. He wore a look that craved everything in sight. He carried a quirt on his wrist that was made of a length of chain sheathed in rawhide, a whip and a bludgeon combined. The butt of a .45 automatic showed under the flap of his chaps pocket. Tom Ford walked up behind Tony's entourage and stood there to support Bill.

"I like that horse you're riding, but I like mine better," Lindano said. "I bet you think that horse is a rope horse. Tomorrow, you and me can match a roping. I'll represent Mr. Claire's outfit, you represent Bradford's."

"This horse is not a rope horse yet," Bill said.

Lindano patted his chaps pocket. "Well, what kind of contest can you handle? A shooting, a riding, a cutting, a chicken pull, a foot race? What can you do?"

"Whatever I decide to do, I want to do it someplace where you can't get behind my back this time," Bill said.

"Have it your own way, but make up your mind. I'm ready. We'll do it tomorrow. I'm riding my top horse. You ride that horse, or any horse. Name your contest."

"We'll cut cattle."

"Bet."

"Two hundred dollars and R.E. holds the stakes."

"Done," said Lindano, and he wheeled his horse and rode away at a lope.

Tony's friends dispersed. Bill and Tom went to the shade and visited with cowboys who had come to join the drive. Now and then they looked up to watch Lindano rein his horse in and out of the trees at a lope. He liked to stop his horse, back him and spur him at the same time, to make him prance. The man was keeping his horse in a lather while all the other horses at the gathering were resting in the shade. The cowboys watched him go by, but none made a comment about him.

Jake and Alex Breach rode in leading a packstring and driving a bunch of big steers. They rode slick horses and were wearing brush-scarred, homemade bull-hide jackets and leggings. They ranched in a rocky, brushy canyon on the edge of the San Augustine Plains. They carried rifles across their laps. Lindano rode by them and they turned their faces away.

"That won't do to take along," said Alex Breach. He was so disgusted by the sight of Lindano that he made no other greeting.

"Don't you like the banker's pet orangutan?" asked Bill, shaking hands with the brothers.

"Watch him."

"I think you should know this Lindano is a bad man," said Jake. "He waters at night in our country. He says he trades horses, but he never stops anywhere with decent people in the daylight."

"We all know him, but he'll be representing the banker on the drive," said Bill. He gave them instructions on where to camp and hold their horses to distract them from talk that might cause a fight with Lindano. They moved their steers to water and then let them drift. They kept watching Lindano in the same way they might watch a wolf that preyed on their stock, as though the wolf had found neutral ground where they could not shoot him. They knew he could slash and cripple, even on neutral ground.

Tom took a crew and went to butcher the cow. Bill rode to the corrals, hitched a team to a wagon, and loaded grain and firewood for the visitors. He tied Steeldust to the tailgate of the wagon and drove the team out of the yard at headquarters. He would leave the loaded wagon under the trees and lead the team back to the corrals. As he drove through the yard, Mary ran out and climbed into the seat beside him. He drove the team past the skinned carcass of the cow. Her ribs were bare and shining in the sun and she was lying on her hide, her ghost long departed. Cowboys helping Tom butcher had uncorked a gallon of whiskey. Bill stopped the team by Cap Maben's fire in the center of the cottonwood grove. Cap spent most seasons camped by himself at Hellsapoppin' Well on the south end of the High Lonesome. He was the cook for the wagon on all the roundups and drives and was in charge of the chuck and hoodlum wagons. Cap had also served in France, and he always wore khaki. He wore a big black hat over his bald head. He made the best sourdough biscuits in Arizona. He was heaping coals and preparing the cow's loin to roast in a Dutch oven. Cap was a cranky man. He laughed only at the misfortune of others. His laugh was the cross between a Bull Durham cough and a rooster's dying wheeze.

Lindano let his horse prance near Cap's fire. Cap looked at him and said, "Now, back that horse off my campground and keep him away from my fire and kettles." Then he turned his back.

"Listen, I'll be guiding these gunsels and the herd to the desert, so you'll be seeing a lot of me, cook," said Lindano. "Get used to a man on his horse. My horse is always with me."

"*You* guide these cowboys to the desert? You? Yes, and I guide redheaded ducks to Montana in the spring. I fly the point myself." Cap laughed and did not turn his face to Lindano.

"Don't joke at me," said Lindano.

Cap mocked him with a high cackle. Hellsapoppin' Well was a camp so far at the end of the High Lonesome that Cap said the sun set between him and all the rest of the humans. He did not care a damn what any man thought of him. He was a cook and he dispensed the groceries to people when he deigned to get near them.

Cap stood up straight and looked Lindano in the eye. "Call it a joke, but I won't tell it again. Keep your dink away from my fire," he said.

Lindano dismounted and tied his horse, then squatted in the shade by Bill's horse. He wanted to be close when Cap's supper was ready. Bill was sure nobody else would invite him to eat.

Bill had tied Steeldust to a tree to keep him away from the grain in the wagon. He poured himself a cup of coffee at the fire.

"What're you going to do about old Sheep Dip?" asked Cap. "You better make him pull up. He's riding his horse to death, tromping the campground, bothering the women and kids, and aggravating the cook."

"I bet you're the only old woman he bothers," said Bill, laughing. "Don't be so jealous of your biscuits. That's all he wants."

Steeldust turned toward Bill's voice and watched him over Lindano's head. Bill took him a morral with a small feed of grain.

"How much for the sorrel?" asked Lindano.

"How much will you give?" asked Bill. He knew that if he priced the horse Lindano would ride him away.

"Is he as sound as he looks?"

"He's sound of body, but probably unsound of mind."

"Since when does a horse need a mind?"

"When a man is not as smart as his horse, the horse needs a mind." Bill laughed.

Lindano studied Bill. He was sure he already knew more about Steeldust than Bill did, because he was a better judge of a horse. "I don't know. I'd have to try the horse before I could decide he suited me. I need a strong horse and a lot of help from the Lord in the work that I do."

"What could you pay for a strong horse that is unsound of mind? I don't know what a horse like this is worth."

"Not much. I'm not rich. I can let you have one hundred eighty-five dollars for him as he stands, saddle and all, I guess. I'm not sure yet that I can use him, but if I can't, nobody can. I make a horse work. He works for me or he dies."

"What would I ride while you were finding out if my horse was worthy of helping the Lord do your work?"

"I brought several mules for the drive. You can have your pick."

"When I want to ride a mule instead of a horse, I'll let you know."

"I can get you a lighter, faster horse that is better trained than this sorrel. Your horse is heavy and slow."

"Far be it from me to mount the banker's foreman on a slow horse. My horse could never meet your high standards."

"I'm willing to take a chance. My offer stands at a hundred eighty-five dollars. You can keep your saddle. It's not to my liking anyway. May the Lord bless your decision."

Bill knew that if he said he would not take less than five hundred dollars, Lindano would dig it up in a moment. He untied Steeldust. "He's not for sale," said Bill, and led his horse to deeper shade.

Lindano followed. "You need a big, fat horse like that, I guess," he said. "That's all you require, a pack horse to carry your carcass."

"Yes," said Bill. "He'd dwarf a man like you."

"I'm not so small a man. I'm stocky built. My heart is

strong. I'll tell you the truth, I had it in a vision. The Lord wants me to ride a big sorrel like this one with stocking hind legs. This horse will sooner or later be mine."

Bill turned away to help measure grain for some visitors. Mary walked up with Tony and began petting Steeldust again. A group was gathering to Cap's biscuits.

Juan Charro, the mountain man, came close to stand beside Lindano. He was tall and raw-boned. His long nose hung over his upper lip. He was wearing homemade leathers. He carried a rifle over his shoulder, muzzle forward so anyone he faced was forced to look into the end of his gun barrel. He had been staring at Bill.

"You taking cattle south this year, Shane?" he asked loudly.

"Yes," said Bill.

"I have cattle." Charro looked around to see if he had an audience. "However, if my cattle are to go, I have to see your money." He lived alone in the mountains in New Mexico, east of the Hellsapoppin', and he was happy to have an audience for his business with Bill.

"You're welcome to throw in with us," said Bill. "But we won't buy them."

"How big a herd are you dreaming up this time, Juan?" asked Cap. "Have you been biting peyote buttons on your mountain again? You own about as many cattle as I do." Cap was the only man Juan Charro saw for months at a time. Charro shifted the weight of his rifle and stared at Cap. The young townsmen laughed. He turned to look at them with eyes as blank as an old house cat's.

"Let's put the horse away, Mary," said Bill.

"Let me ride him back to the corral," said Cap. "Mary can look after my biscuits." Mary handed him the reins. Cap led Steeldust in a circle, looked him over, and mounted. Steeldust turned his head and looked at Cap's foot. Cap kicked him with his heels. He had put away his spurs long ago, when he began cooking for the High Lonesome.

Steeldust took one step forward and two steps backward. His ears went flat against his head and his sides began to swell as though he was about to blow up in a fit of frenzy. The townsmen laughed. Cap smiled wanly, tapped his leg with the tips of the reins and dusted flour off his trousers. Steeldust backed up.

"I guess I won't be riding him after all, Bill," Cap said. "I haven't got time to back him to the corrals and he doesn't seem to want to go any other way. My biscuits'll burn."

Tony sat down by Lindano's feet, unstrapped Lindano's big Chihuahua spurs, and put them on his own heels. Cap dismounted.

"What's the matter, won't he go?" Tony asked, jumping up and taking Steeldust's reins.

"Bill's great horse is stalled in my kitchen," said Cap.

"That horse is having a conniption," said Juan Charro. "I can't stand that."

"He never did that before," said Bill. He was embarrassed. He realized all of a sudden that the horse was so green no one but himself had ever been on his back. Bill did not want anyone else riding his horse, but he had been acting so jealous of him he did not know how he could stop Tony from riding him without acting petty.

"Let me have him," said Tony. "He's just right for a good-lookin' bronc-ridin' type like me. If I can ride him to the corrals and stay purty, I think I'll just buy him."

Bill decided he might as well let the horse make his own way out of the mess. He was supposed to be broke. "Get on him and ride him if you want to," he said. He walked to the base of a tree and sat down. He felt like a traitor, and Tom was looking at him as though he had gone crazy.

Steeldust made no move when Tony mounted him. Tony was big and cocky, full of himself, showing off. "Now we'll see what it is you really want to do, feller," said he. He squalled and jabbed Steeldust with Lindano's spurs.

Steeldust tucked his tail and lurched forward like a truck

jumping out with the brakes on. He came to a rigid stop and turned to look at the boy, showing the white ring of his eye. Tony jerked on one rein and spurred him again. "Look at me, will you?" said he. "Look at you, you wild-eyed cayuse, you."

Steeldust hopped in a circle. He was not yet thinking of bucking Tony off. Tony spurred him in the shoulder and Steeldust threw down his head so hard it whipped from side to side and gave each eye a look at the sky and jerked the reins from Tony's hand. He exploded straight away, kicked high behind and fell on his head, pivoted on his front feet and his nose, then flopped back the way he had come. Tony sailed out into the midst of a bunch of cattle that were grazing near the cottonwoods. He landed on one ear and his head folded under him as he skidded along. His carcass finally came to rest and his hind end straightened off his head, his face emerged, and he smiled. The cattle scattered away and the townsmen all laughed.

Steeldust stared at Tony as though surprised to see the man on the ground in front of him. He backed away and started walking around the man. Mary took his reins and led him to the shade.

"They ought to let me try him again, I guess," said Tony to his friends. "He caught me by surprise." He said it quietly so no one would try to bring the horse back.

"That horse needs a kinder hand, I think," said Juan Charro. "When he bucks, he makes a separate earthquake with each foot."

"Enough is just enough," Mary said. "It's my fault this happened."

"Now, that girl would be the right one to handle your bronco, Bill," said Charro. "You should hire her to lead him home, and if he is all you have to ride, go afoot."

Mary flushed and mounted Steeldust. Her feet did not reach Bill's stirrups. She started the horse away and he broke into a smooth trot without offering to buck. Mary turned back and smiled at Bill. Bill and Tom sat with Tony in the shade.

"Cap's biscuits smell done," said Tom. He was whittling on a matchstick, preparing himself a toothpick.

Cap lifted the lid of a Dutch oven, looked at his biscuits, and carefully put back the lid. "No," said he.

"Well, Tony, you should feel good, now that you're one step closer to being a genius," said Tom, trying to make the boy feel better.

"How's that?" asked Tony, looking at the ground between his knees.

"I know how much it smarts to get bucked off in front of all your friends. All that smarting is bound to smarten a feller."

"I could have rode him, but that flip-flop he pulled threw me off my guard," said Tony.

"Threw you off your round ass, you mean," said Cap.

"How does that Juan Charro make a living, dumb as he is?" asked Bill. "Every time he shows up here, he's collapsing from want and gaunt as a town dog."

"He shows up at Hellsapoppin' ridin' the chuckline all the time," said Cap. "He usually brings me wild honey. He's probably helping somebody steal cattle when he's at my camp watching me. He's been in the joint for rustling, and my neighbors are losing cattle all the time."

"That colt put in a day's work today," said Tom.

"He bucked with me in the pasture this afternoon," said Bill. "Today was the first time he ever bucked. I rode him because I had him bucking downhill. He didn't get a chance to turn back on me like he did Tony."

"He swapped ends just like he'd been drilled for it," said Tom. "That old lion taught him good."

"He'll probably start bucking me off if I fail to meet his high standards too," said Bill.

A small cowpuncher raised up in back of a wagon that had been parked near Cap's fire. He squinted at the sun and stepped carefully to the ground. His thick red hair was hanging in his eyes. He smoothed it with one hand, then covered it up by cocking his hat on the side of his head. He looked into the faces of the cowboys at Cap's fire with blue eyes that were guileless as a child's, but they were bloodshot. The cowboys could see he was unshaven and had not been looking after himself because of drink. He picked a demijohn off the bed of the wagon and set it on the ground, then lifted out his bed, saddle, blankets, and warbag. He laid his outfit under the tree where Bill and Tom were sitting and offered his hand.

"Jonas Ryan," said he. "I call everybody 'honey.' I go by Jonas Ryan everywhere I go. I hear you have work to do with cattle and horses. I never stole or hurried a cow, never abused a horse, nor quit a man in a storm."

Bill and Tom stood and shook his hand. "We do have the work," Bill said.

"Well, honey, when do we start?" Jonas laughed.

"Day after tomorrow, after we've had a little fun."

"That's the kind of outfit I've been a-lookin' for, the kind that celebrates before the work." Jonas handed his jug to Tom. "I have to die or drink more poison. If you have any mercy, you'll help me get rid of the poison before it kills me."

That evening Bill fed Steeldust in a stall. He whistled softly to the horse, then went back to the cottonwoods to see if he could dance with Mary. Alone, Steeldust chewed his hay and grain and watched and listened to the people by the fires. His stall was quiet and the people's doings were carefree and did not intrude on his peace.

CHAPTER 4

A horse helps man out of generosity. A man's grip is too puny to bully a horse into giving him a day's work, but a horse will give himself away until he is poor for the man he has authorized to use him.

A horse can ration his great strength in a long, staying effort to grace a man's work, or he can use himself in an instant of flying hair, tidal hide and burning muscle, glaring eye, flattened ear, and growling voice to put a man on the ground. Any manner in which he uses himself is all the same to a horse, for he is generous.

R.E. Bradford came to the dance at two-thirty in the morning to put his crew to work. Bill was glad to see him. Mary had kept herself close to Tony and their friends through the whole night's celebration. Bill had stayed apart with Tom, Jonas Ryan, Cap Maben, and Jonas's jug, telling stories.

As Bill started away with the crew, Mary came after him, found him in the darkness, and took his hand.

"Time to go to work?" she asked.

"Yeah, but it seems to me this time of day is better play time than work time," said Bill, smiling in the dark. He was thinking he might as well be frowning; Mary never looked at his face when he was wearing an expression she might like.

"You're not saddling Steeldust this morning, are you?" she asked.

"Well, no, he gets to rest until the cutting this afternoon. Just me has to work all day. Give a thought to poor old Bill, why don't you?"

"Can I ride him? I promise I won't even break him out of a trot. I'll just ride him awhile with my friends to loosen him up. It'll do him good. I'll feed, rub, and brush him for you too."

"Take him, but don't pet him." Bill turned to catch up with the crew.

"I know how to take care of him," she said cheerfully as he walked away.

"I don't care what you do with him. Just don't pet him," said Bill.

"Don't worry. You won't worry, will you?" she called, laughing.

Bill went on. The other men were walking away fast and taking hold of the work.

"Bill?" she called once more. He walked on in the dark with the jar of his feet pounding in his ears.

Tom was roping horses when Bill walked into the lamplight of the saddlehouse. The remuda was held in a corner of the corral that was boxed by a rail. The horses stood with their heads sticking out over the rail. Tom was catching them and leading them out as fast as he could build a new loop. He never missed.

Tom assigned Jonas a string of six horses and pointed them out in the dark. He wanted to know in a hurry how good a hand Jonas would make. If Jonas could remember the names and characteristics of six horses assigned him in the dark, he might make a hand. Tom asked Jonas to tell him which horse he wanted to ride that day. Jonas had only seen them skylined against the horizon.

"The buckskin, Bullet," said Jonas. Tom caught the horse and approved of the choice. Bullet was a circle horse, the kind to ride on the wide perimeters of a roundup, smooth of gait and full of stamina.

Bill asked Tom to catch Joker, his circle horse. Joker was a bay with a wonderful running walk and race-horse speed. Bill saddled him, led him through the gate, and mounted.

Jonas was right behind him on Bullet. They waited outside while everyone else saddled and primped and kept an eye on R.E.

After his fashion, when he was ready, R.E. mounted and rode out at at a high trot without looking back. He left without a word or sign to anybody. Anyone who was mounted and ready had to leave. Anyone else was on his own to find his way to catch up.

R.E. rode the perimeter of the big draw and waved his arm when he wanted two men to peel off and drive cattle toward the cottonwoods. He never looked back. As he waved them off, the gang of cowboys behind him dwindled. Finally, everyone had been assigned a drive but Jonas.

Still at a high trot, still not looking back, R.E. arrived on the last plateau above the cottonwood grove. He usually worked that country alone, because it was a wide-open slope with only a short drive downhill to the holdup ground. He expected he had distributed all the cowboys evenly around the pasture.

Jonas had not been told where the cattle were to be found, where they were to be driven, and had not been assigned a partner. Smiling on, he held Bullet in line behind R.E. R.E. had not even spoken when he appeared at the dance.

He let his minions try to read his mind. Everyone had read his mind correctly except Jonas, who had not given a damn what he was thinking.

The sun was coming up. R.E. was deep in thought about weights, measures, cattle markets, bank drafts, and liquid accounts. He figured he was alone, trotting along way out on the High Lonesome. Then, up beside him rode little Jonas Ryan on Bullet.

"I say there, honey, we're a-seein' the country, ain't we?" shouted Jonas, grinning into R.E.'s face. Startled, R.E. almost fell off his horse. He was never very steady on a horse anyway. He suffered from an affliction cowboys called The Roundass. He did not ride on his legs like his cowboys did, and his fanny was round and rolled over his saddle like a ball bearing. Because of this affliction, he seldom rode. Bill and Tom said he rode mostly to use his big saddlehorn for a desk to sign checks and make tallies. After being almost scared off his horse by Jonas, he recovered his balance and rode on, but that was the first time he had ever seen Jonas Ryan and his first indication that Jonas was on his payroll.

Mary and her friends rode out to meet the herd when it came in sight, and by noon the crew held the cattle by the cottonwood grove. The cowboys took turns leaving the herd to catch fresh horses and to stop at Cap's fire for a "dinner" of beefsteak, beans, biscuits, gravy, coffee, and lick.

Bill took Steeldust away from Mary and saddled him for the contest with Lindano. Steeldust was shining like the Mexican sorrel gold coin called the *alazán,* from the washing and brushing Mary had given him.

The visitors' cattle were to be sorted out and a tally made so that R.E. could take delivery for the drive. R.E. never took delivery of his neighbors' cattle until he had cut them away from the herd, seen they were healthy, noted their brands, and tallied a description of the other markings on each hide.

R.E. saddled his cutting horse, Bob Kane. Visitors lined up in the shade to watch. Owners were sitting their horses around the herd. R.E. eased Bob Kane into the herd and began working out a cow and calf. Bob Kane walked carefully, anticipating their direction so he would not have to hurry to put them out. He had to remain quiet so he would not stir up the herd and so he could stay underneath the old cowman with the round ass. Many horsemen at the roundup sat their horses better than R.E., but no horse was better at cutting than Bob Kane. As long as he rode Bob Kane, R.E. was the best in the country, quick and strong as his horse.

Bob Kane cut out thirty-two pairs of cows and their calves without hurrying, breaking a sweat, or drawing a long breath. R.E. stood him away from the herd and brushed his right palm down across the fingertips of his left hand, the Indian sign that he was finished.

Lindano and Bill rode inside the circle of cowboys who were holding the herd. R.E. turned away from Bill and gave Lindano the Indian sign to go first. Fifty head of six- to ten-year-old bulls and steers were to be cut. The cattle were not slow. They were big, active longhorns. Called "natives" by the Arizonans, they were tall and rangy, with horns spreading four to six feet, light of foot and quick to get out of sight. They were cattle that ranged far to make a living and they loved rough country.

Though R.E. and Bob Kane had been quiet in cutting out the cows and calves, the wolfy old bulls and steers were looking way off toward their home ranges, and every now and then one made a dash to test the horsemen holding them. The steers were all renegades who had grown large and wily from years of watching roundups pass them by from icy peaks or brushy thickets. Bulls were turned into cash when they were too old to be of service, but cowmen said any steer was most "merchantable" when he was a yearling. The older and more wily he became, the more "unmerchantable" he was.

To win, Lindano had to cut twenty-five head in less time than Bill cut his twenty-five. He was riding his sorrel, Little Pie. He used a severe spade bit and a death grip on the reins. Little Pie kept a scared eye on Lindano instead of watching the cattle. He pranced about with his head high, slinging froth from his mouth and rattling the cricket in the bit. The cattle might as well have been a herd of boulders through which he was expected to move. He was only concerned that he move fast enough to keep Lindano's quirt off his rump.

Lindano pointed Little Pie at two spotted lead steers belonging to the Breach brothers. They were gentle, as tall as saddle horses and perfectly matched. The Breaches used them as oxen for farming and for leading wild cattle home from canyon, and mountain country. They were used to working in *yunta,* yoked side by side, had been moving in unison all their lives, and were responsible for bringing in many outlaw cattle. They even cocked their heads in the same attitude when they turned to look and listen. Watching Lindano, they raised their dark, wet noses to smell him and his nervous horse. Their heads swung toward the outside as Lindano ran at them with Little Pie. They were used to being separate from the herd and they liked to be apart. Thus, in five seconds Lindano cut two of his twenty-five.

The spotted steers trotted away and were held by the cowboys away from the herd. Lindano pulled Little Pie off their track and swung him back to the herd without stopping the cutter to show he was through with them. That did not matter to Little Pie. He was so afraid of Lindano that he had never seen the spotted steers. Lindano aimed him at a bull on the edge of the herd and ran the bull away from the herd.

In this manner, by running them off the edges, Lindano managed to cut five more bulls and a gentle work ox while he stirred up the herd and made it hard to hold. He sweated and spurred, quirted and jerked on Little Pie. As he rode by Bill and Steeldust, they heard him grinding his teeth.

The job of the cowboys holding the herd was to turn back all the cattle that came at them. They never asked which one the cutter wanted out. The cutter was expected to show them which one he wanted.

At the end, Lindano began running whole bunches toward the outside. The cowboys turned back the cattle that were supposed to stay and let the cuts go out, in effect cutting them for Lindano.

Chasing these bunches, Lindano yelled orders at the cowboys such as "Let that one through. Turn those three back. No, no, let that one go. All right, dammit, let 'em all go. Now bring those three back. That's fine, good work. That's the way." He pointed imperiously at cowboys, cattle, and wide open spaces, like a cattle baron whose big cut was turning out well.

Finally, after an hour, Tom and Jonas rode into the herd, bracketed Lindano's last steer between them, and hazed him out. Bill and Steeldust were faced with an excited herd and twenty-five steers Lindano had chased and been unable to handle. Bill sat awhile and smoked with Tom and Jonas while the herd settled down. Lindano pranced his horse and postured for the spectators at the cottonwoods.

Bill headed Steeldust straight for a brindle steer who had been keeping his head down and hiding like a snake in the middle of the herd. Steeldust locked on his tracks and started him out. When Brindle had an idea he could double back, Steeldust blocked his way and pushed him on. He could not even think of turning back without looking into Steeldust's broad chest. He could not gain on Steeldust. He could not get around him. His vision became so full of the horse that he did not know he was being worked to the edge until he jumped away from the herd. He looked up and saw only open spaces. Steeldust did not let him look back. Then the brindle saw the cattle Lindano had put out, and he threw up his head and ran for them, hunting a friend.

Steeldust had been shown so many cattle in his training that he often knew what a steer would do before he decided to do it. Bill showed him the steers he wanted out and then sat up straight and stayed with him and rode him as well as he could to keep from hindering his work. Steeldust would not wait on Bill, catch him when he fell, or consider his fine seat and dashing figure, as Bob Kane did for R.E. He would buck Bill off if he lost his balance and loosened his seat.

Steeldust was much quicker than Bill to anticipate a steer's direction. Steeldust's laziest reflex made Bill's quickest reaction look slow, yet he never seemed to hurry. The longer he worked the herd, the more it quieted down.

Sometimes, when an animal was outside but had not decided to quit the herd, Steeldust laid back his ears and crouched, head low, nose pointed toward the steer like a sheep dog. When the steer charged back toward the herd, he found he could not make it without running over the twelve-hundred-pound horse. After a hard fight, when a steer had been beaten and run away, Steeldust sometimes raised his head and nickered after him in triumph.

Steeldust cut twenty-five cattle in twenty-five minutes and acted almost lazy when Bill rode him out of the herd. The spectators in the cottonwoods applauded and honked their horns. Tom and Jonas shook Bill's hand. R.E. stopped Bob Kane beside him and pointed his forefinger to the sky in front of his breast, the Indian sign that Steeldust had been superior. Steeldust rested. R.E. handed Bill his winnings.

Lindano worried Little Pie close to Bill. "You didn't beat me by much," he said. "I cut out the wild cattle, so you had only the gentle ones to work."

Bill looked at the chain quirt and at Little Pie. "Anybody could beat Little Pie, the way you ride him," he said.

"He just means you should have warmed up your horse before the contest," said Tom. "He looked cold."

"Listen, I lost this cutting because I've been too good to him. He needs a beating."

"Sure, he probably doesn't get enough beatings," said Tom. "But don't beat him here. Somebody'll make you eat your chain. Better let him rest before he falls over and breaks your leg."

Lindano wanted no fight with Tom Ford. He stared at Steeldust. Steeldust was softly breathing the stink of Lindano, rationing it so it would not shock his system. He watched Lindano and Little Pie with gentle curiosity, wondering why they were so aggravated. Lindano laughed, jerked Little Pie around, and loped away.

Bill helped hold the herd while Tom and R.E. took turns cutting and tallying the rest of the cattle. When they were finished, Bill, Tom, and Jonas rode together to Cap's fire. Mary stepped up to Bill's stirrup before he dismounted and put her hand on Steeldust's shoulder. "Boy, our horse showed that feller the difference between running them off and turning them back," she said. A blush of sunburn was on her tanned cheekbones under her clear blue eyes.

"Here, get on him, Mary," Bill said, dismounting. "We'll take Tom's and Jonas's horses back to the corral for them so they can tap a jug and help Cap pick the beans."

Tom and Jonas were not anxious for Bill to unsaddle their horses, but they could see he wanted to do it so he could take Mary with him. They let him take their horses. Bill mounted Tom's Jon and led Bullet, and Mary rode Steeldust. As they rode toward the corral, Bill watched Mary grace his horse. She was not just being packed along by him. One looked just as fine as the other in the partnership. Mary laid the palm of her hand against the horse's shoulder, patted him and spoke privately to him, and did not say a word to Bill on the way to the corral.

Bill was not much at wooing females. The best he could do for Mary was let her ride his top horse. He did not even realize he was trying to woo Mary. He liked watching her move, so he gave her something to do. He liked sharing his chores with her. He only did that with someone he liked. If he gave Mary something to do it would keep her near and maybe nature would play to bring them closer.

Bill unsaddled the horses and Mary gave them their morrals. Bill had a drink of cool water from the faucet at the water trough and Mary was right there to have one too. Bill went to the long shade on the east side of the saddlehouse and sat against the cool wall. Mary sat down next to him, touching him with her leg.

"I'm going to see if I can buy Lizard, Mary," said Bill, because he could not think of anything more natural to say.

"I didn't know you wanted Lizard," said Mary.

"I can buy him with the money Steeldust won today, if Claire will sell him."

"I'll tell you what we can do. I'll buy him with my money and trade him to you for Steeldust."

"You know how to woo a feller. Just keep telling me how much you like my horse."

"I'm not wooing you. I'm making a simple trade. You get Lizard, I get Steeldust. How'm I wooing you?"

"Mary, you're plotting to get my horse."

"He suits me better than he does you. I want him."

"You want. Since when do you want for anything?"

"You'll give him to me all right. You've been neglecting me. You have to pay for that."

Bill did not want to answer this. He had never gone for child's play. He stood up to close the saddlehouse door. Mary followed him. He knew she wanted to talk. They had both come here for a chance to talk. Bill was thinking, She may still be awful young, but she'll never be any bigger. How old was she? Seventeen? Eighteen? He knew they were both thinking, It's now or never. They had finally broken loose from the crowd together to be alone, and they were already headed back instead of pulling up and talking awhile like they both had come to the corrals to do. Tomorrow Mary would be headed back to school and Bill would be off on the trail to Red Rock with the herd. If Mother Nature wanted Bill and Mary to be together, she'd better hurry up and strike the spark.

"Bill, I have to go back to school tomorrow. Let's not go back to the cottonwoods yet. Let's stay here."

Bill started moving. "Mary, don't cut short your fun. Don't fool with me until you're ready to start your life's work."

"I'm ready. Show me where to start."

"Be patient," Bill said. He knew he had to put a serious end to the talk. He figured everything had its season and it was too late this year for Bill and Mary. He found his legs were carrying him away from the corrals. Mary had flushed him out and run him toward the company, music, and fires.

He kept walking. Mary did not say another word. She turned away to the dark house and was gone.

The neighbor folk were having supper of roast beef and showing off their canning, baking, quilts, and babies at the High Lonesome party. People were dancing in firelight. Tom and Jonas were standing near a fire with their backs against a tree. Bill heard Pete Kapp bragging in a loud voice. He was standing behind another tree with a bottle of whiskey and a herd of townsmen.

"Big talk don't sound that bad when I'm doing it," said Tom.

"I just cain't stand a big mouth nor one who gets rowdy with his whiskey, unless it's me," said Jonas.

Kapp spotted Bill. "Shane, let me give you cowboys a drink," he shouted.

"By Gawd, that's asking for trouble," muttered Jonas.

"How're you boys doin'?" shouted Kapp. "Come on over and have a drink."

Bill started toward him.

"Say, you boys ain't very good horse breakers. We had to throw that roan colt to shoe him and he broke his jaw. Those colts I bought from R.E. ain't broke at all."

Bill walked up to Kapp. "What's that again, Fat Face?"

"You boys don't know much about training horses. We had to throw that Lizard horse to shoe him."

"What's being done for the colt now?"

"What can be done for a broken-jawed horse that nobody can handle? He can't eat. He can't work. We gelded him while we had him down, but he'll starve to death before he heals up."

"Did you have a vet look at him?"

"You're crazy. It would cost more than the horse is worth to have a vet go see him."

"Where is he?"

"At Claire's new Red Rock pens."

"Write him off, then. How much is he worth?"

"I told you, he ain't worth killing."

"Price him."

"Hell, we ought to be paid back what he cost. It's your fault he's crippled."

Kapp turned his back. Bill punched him on the ear with the heel of his hand and his hat rolled on the ground.

"I'm talking to you. Settle with me," said Bill.

"I'll settle with you all right," Kapp yelled. "I can fight, too." He began unbuttoning his shirt. Tom stepped between them.

"Take off your shirt, Fat Man, and I'll stuff it in your ear," Tom said. "There'll be no fightin' in front of all these good people."

"How much for a dead horse?" Bill asked. "Price him, or come off in the brush with me."

"I gave three hundred fifty bucks for him. I want my money back and something to boot."

"How much to boot? How much before I shove your face in?"

"He's worth four hundred, my dollar-a-day buckaroo."

Bill tried to hand Kapp his cutting contest stakes and winnings. Kapp ignored his hand. He had been sure Bill could not pay for enough hair off Lizard's tail to make a hatband.

"Take it and give the man a bill of sale," said Tom. "Or, by God, watch how I make you take it."

Kapp took the money, counted it, grinned, stuffed it in his pocket, and wrote a bill of sale on a tally sheet.

"I'll be sending someone for the horse right quick," said Bill.

"Listen, we'll drag his carcass away where you can find it. Hurry down or you won't recognize it. You just bought a dead horse, sonny."

"Kapp, don't make the mistake of spending my money before I get the horse."

Bill walked away with Tom and Jonas.

"Pard, why did you have to make trouble with the fat man?" asked Tom.

"He's got trouble if my horse dies," said Bill.

"The trouble is, he don't even know he's done wrong," said Tom.

Bill stopped at Cap's fire for his supper and Cap told him R.E. wanted to see him. Bill drank a cup of coffee and walked to the house. He knocked and watched through the window as R.E. raised his head and nodded to him.

"You want a cigar?" R.E. asked, when Bill stepped inside. R.E.'s cigar smelled good, but Bill declined. He did not want to sit back with a big cigar if R.E. was going to drop a hammer on his head. "Sit down in that easy chair. That's a nice, comfortable chair," said R.E.

Bill had never sat with R.E. in his front room. He did not feel put out because of it. He liked R.E., admired him and received good treatment from him. He was happy R.E.'s retreat was comfortable.

"Is everything ready for the drive?" asked R.E.

"Certainly," said Bill.

"I agree. It's time to go. We're strong."

"That's right."

R.E. studied Bill for a long moment. "I want to congratulate you on your colt. That other colt, the one Tom trained, was also a helluva colt. I'm sorry I had to sell him."

"Lizard? He'll make a great horse. I own him now."

"How did you come to own him?"

"Pete Kapp's cowboys couldn't handle him and they broke his jaw fooling with him. I made Kapp price him and I bought him."

"You did just right."

"I think so, too."

"How much was he? I'll buy him from you."

"This time he's not for sale."

"What kind of trouble are you going to have with Lindano on the drive."

"Who knows? He's always got some kind of trouble."

"Don't pay any attention to him. He's just repping for Claire. You and Tom run the drive."

"Sure and it won't be any other way."

"What kind of a deal do you have with Mary? She came in here this evening and asked me to buy Lizard for her. How come she wants that horse, now?"

"We didn't make a deal. Mary said she would see if she could buy Lizard. She wanted to trade him to me for my colt. She has a passion for my horse."

"Oh, she wants *your* horse?"

"Yes, sir."

"How do you feel about that?"

"I'd like to keep my horse, but I'd give him to her if she was more grown up about it."

"You'd give her the horse if she was your sweetheart?"

"I'm not after Mary, if that's what you think. I wouldn't try to buy her with a horse."

"Mary's a finagler. She figures if she shows an interest in your horse, you'll show an interest in her. Isn't that right?"

"Hell, I don't know what phase of the moon she's in, or why she wants anything. She's always fancied the horses I rode."

"Do you want to give the girl a horse?"

"Listen, I don't even like her most of the time, but she can have anything I've got."

"Well, forget about making horse deals with Mary."

"If you say so."

"I say so. Where does that leave us?"

"Hell, I won't mess in your business of raising your kid and marrying her off."

"Good."

"Since you're going South, I was wondering if you wouldn't mind taking Lizard out of Claire's pens and looking after him for me. I'm asking it as a favor, if it won't put you out too much."

"Tit for tat. If you won't make horse deals with Mary, I'll look after your horse for you."

"That suits me."

"I want you to know, I have nothing against you, Bill. I don't want to have any fights over this, no splits and no arguments. Mary has her own friends and I want her happy while she's getting her schooling. She doesn't need to complicate her youth by making horse trades with my cowboys."

"That suits hell out of me."

"Is there anything you need before you start the drive? Anything I can do? Do you need any money? Do you want a drink?"

"Not a thing, thanks," Bill stood up. He had not noticed if R.E.'s easy chair was nice to sit in.

"I won't have another chance to talk to you, for a while," said R.E. "We're driving to the valley tomorrow. I have to put Mary back in school, look at the cattle I have in partnership with Kapp and Claire, see about your horse."

"Have a good trip."

"Well, shake my hand. I have to know you feel all right about this. I am trusting you to get the herd to Red Rock in good shape. I'm partnering with Claire, now. I owe him money. He'll forclose on me if anything happens to that herd."

"Rest easy about it." Bill looked R.E. in the eye and took his hand, but he did not smile as was his habit.

He walked out of the house and looked once at the light shining from Mary's room.

Mary was sitting on a board halfway up the windmill tower and she watched Bill walk back to Cap's fire. She could distinguish his soft voice as he picked up his supper. She enjoyed the voices and firelight and the music from her perch on the tower. Bullbats were gliding in softly and quickly and scooping water off the reflections of the stars in the steel tank below her. She was not going back to the party to tell her friends goodbye before they left for town. She was preparing herself for leaving the ranch.

She climbed down the tower's ladder and walked to the corrals. Until yesterday she had felt happy all the time and she had looked forward to returning to school. She had stayed away from corrals all summer mostly to keep from dirtying herself in the manure, dust, and blood that was not a part of the society of her friends.

Now, Bill had brought her back to the stock. She enjoyed new wonder for animal hips and shoulders, strength and grace. She enjoyed the barehanded way Bill Shane took care of the stock. None of her friends knew how beautiful that could be. She was sorry she had been so conceited she waited until the last day of her vacation to come back to the ranch. She was glad to be back, sorry she had to leave again so soon.

Mary was surprised to find Steeldust in a stall. He raised his head and looked at her when she came near. He watched her intently a moment, saw she was carrying nothing he could coax from her, found nothing untoward about her, turned back to his hay. Mary rested against the stall and laid her hand on his shoulder. The shoulder was tight and hard as the trunk of a tree, but warm and moving and almost hot. Steeldust did not seem at all concerned that she was there, or that anything could be more important than his hay. Mary stayed awhile and felt him gliding still and apart from the world while he fed and rested.

CHAPTER 5

Cuando el arriero es malo, le echa la culpa al macho. When the drover's work is bad, he blames his mule.

ON the drive, the chuckwagon carried provision and utensils for feeding the crew. The hoodlum wagon carried horse-feed, bedrolls, warbags and outfits. The remuda sustained itself by grazing on the country and was grained morning and night.

The cowboys rolled out of their beds when they heard Cap building up his fire and boiling his coffee water before daylight. The nighthawk drove in the remuda, corraled it in a rope corral near the wagon, and Tom caught the crew's mount of horses for the morning.

Bill was using Steeldust at every job he could show him and the horse had not refused to do his best at every job. He was smooth gaited and paced himself well as a circle horse, saw well and was surefooted for his duties as a night horse. He watched cattle day or night. He ate and rested well after any job. He always had the reserve he needed to sprint and turn a cow.

Cowboys making a drive did not ride close enough to talk to one another, though each knew where the others were working most of the time. Bill and Steeldust were most content when they were alone on a drive: looking for cattle, finding them, starting them on their way to the roundup ground, riding the ridges to keep track of them.

One day, Bill rode by a coyote lying dead in the bottom of a wash. The coyote was all by himself, dead under a sheer, sandy bank. As Steeldust passed over the coyote, Bill looked down past his stirrup into the wash and saw him. Steeldust looked at the coyote once and showed no interest in him at all. Bill stopped for a long moment, suspecting the coyote was playing possum, but flies were buzzing at his eyes and nose and he was still as death. Bill rode on. Bill and Steeldust both figured the coyote's reasons for lying dead were his own business.

Bill was in a country called Deep Lake, a dry lake bed in the bottom of a crater a half mile square and a hundred feet deep. The sides of the crater were cut by a badland of gullies and washes where cattle could hide. Bill found no cattle there and he rode out. Returning to the spot where the coyote had been lying dead, he found no sign of the coyote's carcass. The coyote had risen and moved. Steeldust showed no more interest in the spot on the return than he had when the coyote had been lying exposed, surprised in his nap and playing dead. Bill laughed, as he imagined the resurrected coyote must be laughing.

A tall knoll stood on the highest edge of Deep Lake and Bill rode to the top to watch the country for cattle. The morning was still. Bill could see the dust of other cowboys stirring cattle toward the roundup. He could see the wrangler moving the remuda. He saw the chuck and hoodlum wagons on their way to make the noon camp.

Steeldust watched these goings on with intense stillness, shifting his attentions sharply as he kept track of the way of the horses, his matchless friends. The wagons were being pulled by eight horses and carrying his morral and his grain. He always wanted to know where that hoodlum wagon was. He poised himself to listen so that not even the saddle creaked unless Bill moved. Bill could hear nothing but the ringing in his ears.

A herd of antelope was resting in the sun below the knoll,

also intent on the sound of the wagons. Beyond the antelope, Bill saw a bunch of cattle. The two Breach lead oxen were with them. The Breach oxen were supposed to be with the main herd. Bill rode off the knoll toward them. The antelope were in Steeldust's path and they remained unaware of the man and his horse.

Steeldust was still listening with his heart in the direction of the wagons when he drew so close to the antelope that Bill could smell their crisp, musky hides.

The buck who was boss of the herd whirled to stare at Bill, then moved broadside across Steeldust's path, alarming the herd with his attitude as he kept his attention on Bill. The herd mustered and leaped away in a long, dashing stream. It changed pace and made a winding turn away, then flashed the white rumps at Bill in unison as it veered away from the cattle. The antelope seemed to move leisurely, running with content and conceit, as they streamed toward the open draw where the wagons were rolling. Bill rode to the chore of the cattle ahead, but watched the antelope until they had dashed in front of the teams and coasted out of sight. Bill was thinking that if it were not for their conceit, no predator in the world would ever have caught an antelope.

The Breach oxen were supposed to be with the main herd, not away in the country that had not been gathered. Bill started some of the cattle he had sighted from the knoll. They lined out into the open and he saw he did not have the Breach oxen. He rode to a high point and still did not see them, so he cut for their tracks. When he found their tracks he saw they were being hurried straight out of the country by someone riding an unshod horse.

Bill pressed Steeldust into a lope, following the tracks in sandy ground. He slowed to a walk when he thought he was near the oxen. He did not want to run up in a big hurry and surprise someone into shooting him. He rode to the top of a ridge, keeping cedar cover between himself and the path of the oxen. The oxen poked into sight from a thicket. The man who was driving them was riding a black, paint mustang. He was moving at a trot and prodding them with a long, sharp stick. The mustang was eager in his work. Bill smiled. The rider was Juan Charro. Bill had never seen him so intent on work. He was headed toward his mountain with the prize oxen of his neighbors, Jake and Alex Breach.

Bill loped ahead and waited in the bottom of a draw. Juan Charro came over the ridge above him, looking back over his shoulder for pursuit. The oxen trotted down off the ridge to Bill and stopped to rest. Juan Charro looked down at Bill and Charro's mustang stopped still, as though he also knew he had been caught stealing cattle.

Juan Charro dismounted and began repairing a stirrup leather, standing on the side his rifle was scabbarded. He kept his back to Bill.

Bill rolled a cigarette. "Where are you headed with the fine oxen of Jake and Alex Breach, Juan Charro?" he asked. Juan Charro appeared intent on tying his stirrup leather together.

"To the roundup," he finally said.

"But the roundup is the other way, Charro," Bill said, smiling.

Charro looked over his horse's neck at free mountains far away. "So it is," he said. "I must have turned east when I thought I was turning west."

"You must have."

"It's a good thing I ran into you, since you seem to know the way to go."

"Come on, you can help me drive them back—so you'll know, too."

Charro mounted his mustang and helped Bill start the oxen toward the roundup. He did not look at Bill.

"It sure seems funny to me you were headed exactly the wrong way," said Bill.

"I must have been confused," said Charro.

"Confused in your own favor. You were on the way to

your mountain and looking *back* so you wouldn't make a wrong turn," Bill said and laughed.

Juan Charro remained silent.

"Didn't you see the wagons when you looked back? Every living thing on the High Lonesome knows when the wagons are moving."

"I didn't see them. I'll tell you, I was going to work the oxen and return them."

"Oh, you asked the Breach brothers for permission to work their oxen?"

"No, I couldn't find them. This is a big ranch. I knew they wouldn't mind. The oxen strayed from your herd and I needed them, so I just pushed them along the way they were going. The Breaches are good neighbors."

"Ah, well, it might matter. You better ask them."

"I think I'll just help you start them and then head for home."

"No, you might as well join the crew. Cap needs a swamper. I know you get along with Cap." Bill figured the best way to keep track of Juan Charro was to put him to work.

Bill looked up and saw Lindano sitting a mule on a ridge, watching him. Bill waved to him. Discovered, Lindano rode to him. He was carrying a rifle across his lap.

"*Ola,* Juan Charro," said Lindano. "Aren't you Mr. Charro who lives on yonder mountain?"

Juan Charro only nodded to him. Bill and Juan Charro were both watching the rifle. Lindano had an amiable look on his face. Bill could not imagine him being amiable about anything unless he was about to kill it, or beat it with his chain.

"I thought you knew each other," said Bill. He was positive they knew each other. The Breach brothers said Lindano haunted the country around Juan Charro's mountain.

"Only by reputation," said Lindano.

Juan Charro was not looking to the right or to the left.

He stayed with the oxen, riding along as though he was being driven as well as they.

"Juan Charro is coming to work as swamper for Cap," said Bill. "Isn't that right, Juan Charro?"

Charro rode ahead with the oxen. He and his mustang had lost the eagerness they had been enjoying before Bill caught them. The oxen walked around the point of a hill and met the remuda grazing in a draw.

Boots Vail was wrangling and he looked up with a cranky nod when Bill called to him.

"You fellers are sure workin' hard, three of you gathering two old oxen that strayed," Boots observed, softly. He would never know how glad Bill was to see him. Lindano put his rifle away. Bill kept the oxen near the remuda. Boots moved the horses toward the roundup so the crew could change horses at noon.

At a moment when the remuda and the oxen trotted down a hill toward the dust and activity of the roundup, Bill stopped Steeldust beside Juan Charro. Boots and Lindano kept trotting ahead.

"You're coming to work, thief," Bill said softly.

Charro looked down at his hands on his saddlehorn.

"I'm not going to say anything to the Breach brothers, yet. You can stay and work for Cap, or Tom will take you to the sheriff. You choose. I won't have a thief worrying the flanks of this herd. You stay and help, tell the truth, don't steal, make a hand—or explain yourself to the sheriff. I bet he can keep you out of our hair until the herd is out of the country."

Juan Charro sighed, smiled, looked Bill in the eye and nodded. They rode down to Cap's fire together. Juan Charro dismounted and walked up to Cap and shook his hand.

Bill ate his dinner, watered Steeldust and cooled his back, and then put him back to work. He cut out cattle that were too weak to make the drive and let them stay to shift for themselves on the High Lonesome. He and Tom roped the calves that had been born since the Spring branding and dragged them to the fire for branding and earmarking.

Steeldust was learning that slack in the rope gave a mean momentum, jerk and haul to the animal whipping on the end. He was handling himself quietly no matter which side of him Bill handled the rope. He held the rope tight on the critter when Bill was on the ground. He faced the calf on the rope and backed up when the calf moved toward him. He learned to drag or "log" a heavy steer when Bill was on the ground, to keep the steer from finding his feet while Bill tied him. He gave no slack unless Bill mounted him and rode him up to slacken the rope. He was trained to never let cattle up when Bill was on the ground, never allow himself to be led by the taut rope on the saddle horn.

This management of the tight rope was a discipline that showed he conquered his natural fear of a taut rope. He worked the rope as an individual doing a man's work, not a horse. If he ever panicked, he could wind his rider in the rope and cut off a limb, or drag him to death. As a horse, he was expected to panic from a taut rope—until he had learned from the man not to be afraid.

As Bill worked through the afternoon, he kept his eye on Juan Charro. Every time he looked up from his work to see if Juan Charro was making a hand, he caught Lindano watching him, watching Steeldust, speculating. Bill was not worrying about Juan Charro, or Lindano. He was worried about the wranglers, Boots Vail and Tony Claire. Bill had been trying to figure why Boots was giving him cranky looks. He could only believe Boots was cranky because he was having to nursemaid Tony Claire.

Boots was the wrangler and Tony was the nighthawk, though they were supposed to trade off periodically. Tony looked after the remuda at night. During the day, he was supposed to help Cap around camp and drive the hoodlum wagon and help hold the main herd when it was being worked. He was allowed to sleep in his spare time. With Juan

Charro working as swamper, Tony would get more rest. And
Boots would get more rest because sometimes when Tony
had trouble nighthawking he would awaken Boots for help.
Once, he had awakened Boots for help and had crawled into
Boots' blankets and gone to sleep as soon as Boots was doing
his job. He called on Boots more than he did the coffee pot
when he was riding nighthawk.

Bill had hired Boots as a wrangler and Boots wanted to
cowboy. Boots was the kind of young man who would kill to
cowboy and he tended to harbor mean feelings for any man
who kept him from it. He was from good stock, but he was
quick-tempered and believed he was smarter and tougher
than everybody else. He was also positive that he could ride,
rope and shoot better than everybody else. He knew his way
around a cow camp and other cowboys. He was too good a
cowboy to be wrangling, but he was the youngest man on
the crew beside Tony and he had been hired to wrangle
because that was the last job Bill had to give him.

Bill let Boots and Tony do a share of the cutting and
roping, but Tony's work was pitiful. He could throw a rope
and he sat his horse well, but when he rode up to help work
cattle he did not know which end of the cow to head so she
would turn. He barely knew the difference between a cow
and a bull and could not tell one from the other if they stood
side by side across a canyon from him. He was further
handicapped because three of the mounts his father and
Lindano had furnished him were old mules who had never
seen a cow in their lives. The first time he rode his dun mule
to turn a cow, the mule shied, swapped ends and ran straight
away from the cow, as though the cow was a black hole in
the ground in which was hiding a spook who was after his
mortal liver. If by accident Tony knew where he ought to be
to turn a cow, he seldom could get his mule there in time to
do it. Once in a while Bill and Tom furnished him with two
gentle High Lonesome saddle horses so that he could be on
an even footing when he tried to make a hand.

Lindano also rode mules. He was so bad with cattle and horses that Bill and Tom left him to his mules so they could keep him out of the way. Little Pie was the only horse in his string.

The evening Juan Charro joined the crew, Cap camped his wagons at the hogan and windmill of Hellsapoppin' Well. When the crew began riding in for supper, Jonas unrolled his bed and dug out a gallon jug of whiskey.

"What's that for?" asked Bill. He never allowed whiskey on the wagon. He looked quickly at Tom. Tom was grinning.

"This awful jug has been a painful cross for me to bear," said Jonas. "I've been scared someone was going to catch me with it and it's too heavy and big to hide in my bed for a sleeping partner. I know it's against the law to bring it on the wagon, so if it's all the same to you fellers, I'll pour it on the ground before it tempts anyone else." He paused a minute to see if Bill might give special instructions to save the whiskey. Bill had no such intent. "However, there's enough thirsty cowboys here, if we all drank an equal share, this little jug wouldn't be enough to cause any serious trouble," Jonas added.

Jonas dug into his bed again, pulled out a harmonica and tooted the scale. "Now, if this old harp can put some of us in the right mood, we might not have to pour good whiskey on the ground."

Bill laughed. "Pour it anywhere you want," he said. "But be damned sure there's none left after supper." He found a cup and poured a swallow for himself. Jonas began playing, *Ah, Sweet Mystery of Life At Last I Found You.* Bill appreciated that Jonas was no sneak. He could have hidden the jug and nipped at it through the drive.

Tony's share of the liquor made him feel tough and he began howling. He pulled his pistol and fired, scattering pigeons roosted under the eaves of the barn. The herd jumped and ran with the shot and the cocktail guard worked fifteen minutes turning them back and quieting them. The shooter was far enough away from the pigeons and the cattle that he had not done much harm.

Tony watched the cattle with a grin on his face and no apologies.

Cap liked the pigeons and shooting them did not suit him. He liked order in his camp. He was not even allowing the crew to use his hogan at Hellsapoppin'. He watched the pigeons hurry in a circle overhead.

Bill waited to see how much trouble the boy would make for himself. No one on the crew was worried by his behavior, so far.

Tony screamed, waved the pistol and yelled, "I'm a dusty, crusty, old trusty cowboy, by damn, I am."

Jonas laid down his mouth harp and squatted near Tony while the pigeons circled closer. Tony grinned and took aim as they settled to their roosts. Cowboys under the muzzle of the .45 scattered for cover, laughing. Tony's wrist was whiskey limp as he let the pistol explode again. Jonas watched the pistol recoil, followed it with his hand and buffeted it between Tony's eyes. Tony was sitting with the back of his head against a wagon wheel and it did not cushion the blow. He twitched, stretched out on the ground and found peace with his whiskey in coma.

Jonas took the pistol, removed the clip and ejected the round from the chamber. He stuck the pistol in Tony's belt and dropped the clip in his shirt pocket.

Bill mounted his night horse and rode out to help the guard quiet the cattle again. He saw Lindano lay Tony on his bedroll and cover him with a blanket. He saw Lindano take the pistol out of Tony's belt and the clip out of Tony's shirt pocket. Bill did not care what happened to the pistol as long as Tony did not shoot it again, but no one should take another man's pistol, especially before the man had learned to use it.

Lindano looked around to see if anyone was watching him

and then looked to see what Bill was doing. Bill figured he had used Tony's mishap to his own advantage in some way.

Lindano had chosen a place to sleep away from everybody else under a grove of sycamore trees where buzzards roosted and stood sentinel for carrion. Lindano did not notice the rich accumulation of buzzard soil under the tree when he laid his bed there after dark. No one in the crew thought enough of him to tell him about it, figuring he would find out for himself in the morning.

Long before dawn, the crew breakfasted and saddled horses, but Tony slept on. Busy cowboys walked by his head, stepped over him, stumbled on him while they prepared to move the herd away from Hellsapoppin' and they still did not disturb his innocent repose.

Bill was saddling Joker for the morning circle when Tony stumbled by and discovered that no one had left him coffee. The fire was dead, the coffee grounds were in a pile by the coals and the coffee pot had been loaded in the chuckwagon. Cap was talking to his team, about to drive away and did not answer Tony's complaint that he could not go to work without coffee. A big lump had formed a prow between his eyes and he could not see well past this swelling.

Tony wandered around the campground, confused at the activity going on without him. The crew left no sign it had rested there. Tony was its only noticeable residue. He mothered up to Lindano when he caught him rolling his bed under the sycamores.

"Mahout, what shall I ride?" he asked.

"Suit yourself, but you better get moving," said Lindano. "We'll be out of sight in five minutes."

"Maybe I could catch up. I have an awful hangover and there's no coffee."

Tony paused where he stood, waiting for some consideration from his father's employee. Lindano turned his back, threw his bed into the hoodlum and struck out for his saddled mule.

Tom was almost finished catching horses when he saw Tony wandering his way. He reached out with a long houlihan loop, caught the dun mule and held him outside the corral while Tony searched for his bridle. A cowboy found the bridle on the ground where Tony had dropped it the night before. He bridled the mule for Tony and tied him near the hoodlum wagon. The dun mule was jumpy and wary of Tony's anxious state as the boy came near him.

Bill mounted and led the circle crew away from camp. He stopped on the last high point in sight of the Hellsapoppin' windmill. He looked back while the horses blew and their heartbeats settled. Tony's dun mule was tied to the corral and dancing in place, impatient to be gone with everybody else. The remuda had been driven away by Boots. The hoodlum wagon had been driven away by Juan Charro. The herd and its dust was long gone with the sound of its bawling. The herd would noon at a camp called Witch Wells. Bill could see Tony wandering and searching by the door of Cap's hogan. Every other man on the outfit was working, but Tony was still looking for some little sugar he needed to comfort his day.

"The boy is having himself a time," Tom said.

"Like a vacation for him," Bill said. "I'm glad to see he's resting well and we had Juan Charro to ride nighthawk for him last night."

Lindano looked humorlessly down at Tony, then at his own mule.

"Another minute and Tony'll be in a world all his own, for sure," said Tom.

"He knows to track the herd and come on, doesn't he?" asked Bill.

Nobody answered.

Bill rode on. At midmorning, he went in with his first drive of cattle and saw Tony riding drag on the herd. Bill joined him. Tony looked worn out from all the catching up he had done. He rode over close to Bill. Bill wanted to talk to him but Tony began riding between Bill and the herd as though Bill were not even there. After his third pass in front of Joker, Bill whacked the dun mule on the rump with the double of his rope and sent him bucking and humping out of his way.

"Hey, you," muttered Tony, hanging on tight.

"Cut me off like that again and I won't waste my whacks on your mule," said Bill. "I'll rope you off him and drag you clear out of sight."

"Dammit, I have to do the work," said Tony.

"Dammit, if you can't make a hand, at least learn some manners. Don't ever ride between another man and the herd. You don't have to do my work. That's why I'm here, to look after this part of the herd."

Tony gave Bill a dirty look and turned away. He did not stay angry at Bill for long. He rode a few steps and began to admire his own figure on horseback by watching his shadow on the ground.

That evening, Bill was walking to the fire after giving Steeldust his morral and Tony stepped in front of him and cut him off from the coffee pot.

"Where's my pistol?" demanded Tony.

"I have no idea," said Bill.

"You took it."

"I didn't take your pistol. Jonas made you eat it before you went to sleep."

Cap laughed.

Tony held a plate of food in his hand. He glared at Cap, threw the plate on the ground and spat. "Nobody can put up with thieves and eat your slop, too," he said.

Cap glared back at Tony. "Pick up the plate," he said. His pale eyes were as fierce as the sawback bayonets he had seen thrust at him on the Argonne. He picked up a stick of split cedar wood.

Tony ignored him and shouldered by him insolently. Instead of stepping aside, Cap whacked him with the firewood behind the ear as he went by. Tony hit the ground on his face and lay still. The crew went on with supper. Tony stirred and began to cry softly with his face hidden against the ground. The cowboys were all looking at Cap's supper on their plates. Tony sat up and wiped his eyes. Bill had a tear in his own eye for the boy. Tony touched the sore place behind his ear and almost cried again.

Cap stood over Tony with a cast-iron skillet in his hand. "You want to feel good again, button?" Cap asked. "Pick up your plate and put it in the wreck. Start washing the dishes. Clean that food off the ground so the skunks and coons won't come and disturb our rest in the night."

Lindano was sitting on his bed and watching, as though waiting to see if anyone would accuse him of having the pistol. He saw Tony stand and put his plate in the "wreck," or dishpan, clean up the food and start washing the dishes. Lindano lay down and turned his face away from the fire.

After awhile, Tony poured himself a cup of coffee and sipped it a moment and then went back to his chore.

Bill felt sorry Tony's lessons were so hard on him. Bill believed if a man insisted on carrying a pistol, he was bound to learn lessons on how and when to use it, how to keep from losing it, and not to blame others when he lost it. Without the lessons, he could not learn the proper rules for carrying a pistol. Tony's lost pistol was giving him so much trouble that maybe he would learn to keep it holstered when it was returned. He might even come to believe he was better off without it.

CHAPTER 6

In flight, a horse launches himself and flies off his hind legs, reaches with head high, locks his front legs ahead of him, lands all his mass on one rigid front leg and then the other, vaults over his front legs like a pole vaulter, then launches again. Because of the slenderness of his structure, his running becomes almost suicidal, yet his grace transcends the physics and saves him. Still, a horse will sometimes break a leg to keep from trampling another living, breathing creature in his path.

THE High Lonesome roundup was over and the herd began to raise dust south, away from lifetime haunts, through the Hardscrabble, the Hinkson and the Platte ranches. They crossed the Little Colorado, passed between Concho Village and the Mesa Redonda, walked through the tinder-dry Ponderosa forest of the White Mountains and off the Malpais escarpment of the Mogollon Rim. On the fifteenth day of the drive, the herd watered at the junction of the Black River, the White River and the Salt River, west of Fort Apache.

Bill, Tom and the wranglers drove the remuda to Cedar Canyon where the horses would be held while all hands worked at fording the Salt River with the cattle. Before the remuda began the descent into Cedar Canyon, Bill and Tom left it and rode down to the camp of their friend, Pascual Matus, the Yaqui.

Pascual was a *Cacique,* chief, from Cajeme in Sonora who came to hide from time to time with the White Mountain

Apaches. He had fought as a scout with the Mexican General Alvaro Obregon through two revolutions and now Obregon had declared him an outlaw. He was one of three Yaqui chiefs who were wanted dead by the Mexicans. The Mexican Cavalry in that year, 1926, still hunted Yaquis, ran them down, killed them and cut off their ears for the bounty.

Pascual made good mescal, caught wild horses and raised cattle with the Apaches. Horses were in great demand in Sonora.

In the generations of fighting between the Indians and the whites in the Southwest, Pascual's family had befriended the Apache and sheltered him in Sonora and had been sheltered by him in the White Mountains. Old Apaches who had been in the Sierra Madre with Geronimo still came to visit Pascual in Cedar Canyon. Pascual was fierce in his love of the Yaqui, his land, and his Catholic faith and he was admired by the Apache who had embraced the peace under the American Government, but still longed for the fight.

Bill and Tom rode down the bottom of Cedar Canyon and saw fresh mule tracks on the trail. Bill hoped they would surprise the Yaqui in his mischief of making bootleg mescal. They came upon a pipeline of bamboo poles laid as an aqueduct down the canyon from a spring. The bamboo had been cut length-wise in half, laid end to end, and propped above the ground to serve as a canal for clear water required at a still. Bill and Tom followed the bamboo and smelled the cooking mescal. In a clearing, they rode by vats laid in the ground where mescal pulp was fermenting.

"Don Pascual Matus of Cajeme," Bill shouted. "Show yourself."

"*No está.* He is not here," a deep, grouchy voice answered from inside the brush close behind them.

"Show yourself, Yaqui," said Bill. He spun Steeldust on his hind legs to show him off.

Pascual stepped out carrying a long, well-honed machete. He was tall, muscular, hard and dark as the heart of mesquite. Bill and Tom dismounted and Pascual came forward. He was wearing *huaraches* and dragging his spurs behind his bare heels. Worn, leather leggings hugged his legs. He took the reins of the horses, led them to the shade and loosened their cinches. He looked hard at Steeldust, then away, hard again, and away again. After he laid corn in separate places for the horses, he stood back to admire them. He considered open admiration and discussion of his friends' horses his courteous duty.

"Tom, I see you still ride the big, cranky sorrel," said Pascual. "Jon of the pigeon toes. The big drivers on the hind end keep the crooked toes out of the way, no, Tom?"

"That's it," said Tom.

Pascual moved around Steeldust. He stopped in front of the horse and pushed his hat to the back of his head. He stood still with his legs braced. After a while he said, "You ride in on this horse while I'm at work, catch me sweating on my bare feet, with only a mule to ride home, and I bet you expect friendship from me. I warn you, I'm a Yaqui, but I have the heart of a horse thief. I watched you all day yesterday from the peaks. I thought the distance was deceiving me. Now that I see him close, I beg you, sell him to me before I cut your throat for him."

"I guess you mean it," Bill said. "I never heard you say so much in one breath."

Pascual reached inside a hut by the still and brought out a jug of mescal. "Drink," he said.

Bill smelled the corncob cork, drank a swallow and handed it to Tom. Tom sipped it and handed it back to Pascual. Pascual drank four big swallows, held the last mouthful, rinsed his mouth and swallowed it.

"Drink it like that," he said. "It's only average. I have some good stuff buried under the snubbing post in my corral. Angry cattle have been dancing over its head for years. That's the stuff you'll like for the taste."

The three men sat in the shade and sipped mescal. Every

once in a while Pascual praised something new he liked
about Steeldust. Finally, he said, "All my life I've wished for
a horse like this. Now I find I won't own him after all. I have
to be content that it is my friend who rides the best horse I
ever saw."

"Let's talk business, Pascual," said Bill, embarrassed. He
felt he had again been made a gift of his horse.

"Speak," said Pascual.

"Will you come and help us with the herd? Can you go to
Red Rock with us and maybe on to Sonora, as you have
before?"

"Yes, I want to go."

"If it rains, R.E. will want us to take the herd across the
border to the coast at Libertad and pasture on Indian wheat
this winter."

"I'll go."

"What about the government? Are you wanted? I know
you are 'Much remembered,' as they say. They probably
want your head on a pole down there, as usual."

"I'm always wanted, by those who would kiss me and by
those who would hang me. It's time for me to go home."

"I don't want to see your countrymen cut off your ears
and hang you to make sure you go deaf."

"I have enemies here, too. Nowadays no one likes the
Yaqui. I'll just pack my mules and go. My cattle will multiply
and my rock corral will be here when I return. I'll throw my
horses in with yours."

"We want to corral the remuda here, as usual."

"Where is it?"

"Coming into the canyon about now."

"Let's go see it."

Pascual led a bronc mule out of the brush where he had
hidden him. He used a *tapojo*, a leather blindfold attached
across the brow of his bridle. The blindfold could be lowered
when he did not want the mule to see that life, according to
Pascual, might be too awful for him to understand. He

hobbled the mule, blindfolded him, saddled him and threw a large mantle of leather called *armas,* arms, over the saddlehorn. When the *mantle* was spread, it covered the mule from shoulder to flank, and protected Pascual's legs and bare toes from the brush. He pulled down his hat, tightened its string under his chin, said, "In the name of God," and stepped on the mule. He reached down and loosed the knot that released the hobbles. The mule began to dance under the blindfold. Pascual raised the blindfold. The mule turned his head and looked at him. Pascual laughed in his face and the mule recoiled, bawled, whirled and bucked away down a trail through the brush.

Bill and Tom followed through a tunnel in the brush that Pascual had cut to use as a hidden avenue to his still. Long before Bill and Tom emerged from the brush, they heard dogs barking and Pascual's laughter as he burst into his camp. He was sitting under a cool ramada when Bill and Tom rode in sight. An aged uncle of Pascual's was sitting by him playing him a battle march on a fiddle.

Pascual's camp was under tall cottonwoods. A rock wall two feet wide and six feet high spanned the canyon. A snubbing post was planted in the center of the corral.

Pascual pointed with his chin—Bill turned and saw the leaders of the High Lonesome remuda appear on the trail at the top of the canyon. Pascual pointed to a Yaqui horseman who was riding ahead of the horses, guiding them and holding them to his pace.

"You see, I knew you were coming and I sent my man to help," said Pascual.

The trail was narrow on the canyon wall. The horses were contained by the steepness and by the lead horseman. The horses streamed down the wall into the canyon, crossed the creek at the bottom and trotted through the gate of the corral. The leaders were chewing on Pascual's cornstalk fodder in the corral before the last of the horses started off the top of the canyon.

The *vaquero* who led the remuda was called Chapo. He carried a Mauser rifle and a bandoleer of cartridges over his shoulder. Pascual's uncle played his march while the remuda streamed into the corral.

Boots and Tony and three other cowboys from the herd brought up the drags, leading pack horses loaded with grain and morrals. Boots and Tony unsaddled, unpacked and laid their gear in the shade of the corral. The sun was setting on the canyon wall. The cowboys drank cool water from an *olla* hanging in a cottonwood and relaxed a moment before they headed back to the herd. Bill introduced them to Pascual. Pascual gave them a cup of mescal to pass around and stood ready to refill it. Chapo and Pascual's uncle went to a big stack of cornstalks by the corral and began throwing bundles of the fodder to the horses. The cowboys helped them finish, then mounted and waved and rode back to the herd.

A fat steer ambled into the clearing and Pascual wanted him butchered. Bill mounted Steeldust, roped the steer around the horns and dragged him to a tree in front of Pascual's wikiup. Pascual stepped out from behind the trunk of the tree and plunged his knife through the steer's jugular. The steer filled his tracks with blood in seconds, then went twitching to the ground. Bill rode up, coiling his rope. Pascual took the bloody loop off the steer and handed it to Bill. He bent and opened the steer's throat from ear to ear so he would bleed freely. Bill rested the loop neatly on its coils over his saddlehorn.

"It's a good thing you didn't cut my rope, Pascual," Bill said. "This rope never misses. I don't know what I'd do without it."

"I was careful," said Pascual. "That manila should be mine for not cutting your throat and stealing your horse."

Bill handed him the rope. "That is a fair reward," he said. Pascual hung the rope over his forearm and watched the steer bleed.

The cowboys hoisted the steer by his heels under the

cottonwood and butchered him. While they were working, Pascual's uncle roasted the liver and kidneys on a mesquite fire and carried them on hot tortillas to the cowboys. Pascual and Chapo dug out a jug by the snubbing post. The cowboys drank mescal and ate broiled tenderloin, beans and corn tortillas, and then went to bed.

An hour before dawn, Bill awoke and went to find Pascual. He found him sitting under a cottonwood against the wall of the canyon. He was slicing the fresh meat into sheets for jerky. He had taken Steeldust away from the other horses and was feeding him corn and talking to him. He had a fire and the horse was standing as close to the flames as Pascual.

"He's not a human to be fed so near while you work, Pascual," said Bill. "He'll step on you."

"He must be kept apart and watched closely, like a woman, or a pistol," said Pascual. "He is not ordinary. He is the gift God gives a good man once. Every worthy man should have one good horse, one woman and one weapon of which others would be jealous."

Bill wrapped himself in his blanket and sat against the base of the tree.

"Your horse honors me," said Pascual. "Something good is happening to me, for a change."

"Where did you leave your family?" asked Bill.

"We were separated in a fight at Vicam. We bronco Yaquis had gathered there to meet with Obregon's parrot, Elias Calles. We were having a fiesta. My wife took our children to the brush, to gather the fruit of the *hecho*. My oldest son and I were with the committee welcoming Calles. Then his Cavalry threatened us and we stood to fight. The Cavalry ran around us and cut through the women and children at the fiesta—hurt many helpless people. I wet my machete well before I left, but if I had been well mounted, I could have rejoined my family. I left there afoot while the Cavalry was trying to regroup. They chased me all the way to the border and I didn't try to shake them off. I had them all on my tail so everyone else in the committee was able to return home."

"*Ai, Yaqui,*" said Bill. He looked to see how Tom was getting along. The man was still in his blanket.

A fire began to glow on the rim of the canyon and it quickly grew into a bonfire. Bill looked away from it so he could keep his night vision.

"Who is doing that?" Bill asked.

"Someone probably waiting for dawn so they can walk down," said Pascual.

Someone by the fire let out a long, mocking howl. Horses began to stir in the corral. Before Bill and Pascual could untrack, they heard a scream and the muzzle blasts of three pistol shots torched the inside of the corral. Pascual ran toward the corral. The horses were pouring out the gate. Bill bridled Steeldust and mounted him bareback. Pascual ran along the top of the rock wall to the gate where the horses were bunching for an instant before streaming out. He jumped to the back of a horse and disappeared in the mainstream of the stampede. The leaders turned down the canyon.

Boots and Tony ran to the gate and waved their arms to try to stop the last horses breaking out. Tom sat up in his blanket, put on his hat, waved goodbye to the remuda and smiled as Bill ran by.

Bill ran Steeldust in among the horses at the tail end. He steadied the horse's head, grabbed his mane in both hands and let him run. The canyon reverberated with the clatter and rattle of shod hooves while someone by the bonfire was firing into the canyon and someone in the camp was returning fire. The shoes of the running horses were striking long sparks along the solid bed or rock.

Bill could not see enough to protect himself. Steeldust was flying, and Bill could only trust to the horse's vision and instincts in the herd. The herd was poised as a body to react to the reflexes of the horses in the lead and on the flanks.

The herd instinct was forcing the path of each horse. Steeldust was absorbed in keeping pace with the remuda and striding recklessly over the smooth river rock. Each new stride was part recovery from having just made a landing on unknown ground and part urgent leap to catch up.

Bill thought of Pascual riding with nothing but a mane hold. Steeldust had outrun the drags and was close to the leaders, but Bill had not located Pascual. The remuda began to slow down. Bill saw riders on the flanks and in the drag. A rider was in the lead holding the pace. Just before dawn, the horses were stopped. The thieves began to speak to one another.

"Pascual?" a man on a flank inquired. "Did anyone see him?"

"No," the man in the lead answered.

"I bet he was full of beef and sleeping with the mescal."

"Don't believe it."

Bill smiled. He was sure Pascual was listening and had located all the riders, unless he had been trampled into a grease spot on the stream bed.

"And the *Yoris*, the whites?" asked the horse thief on the flank.

"Those won't bother us," said the horse thief in the lead. "They're afoot and their feet are too soft for the rock."

The two horse thieves laughed gently.

Another deep voice laughed softly near Bill, below the echo of the voices in the canyon. Bill located four horsemen on the perimeter of the remuda. He rode Steeldust off the edge of the herd and hid him in shadow, brush and boulders. He dismounted, rested and waited. He had come off without his pistol.

The thieves were not doing any bragging. They were still wary of their back trail.

As soon as the light allowed it, the rustlers started the remuda down the canyon again. The stream bed fell off steeply and was so full of rock and water that the horses were often forced to swim when sheer rock blocked the way. The rustlers were speaking Spanish. They were Yaquis, or Mayos, not Apaches. They dismounted and turned loose their mounts and herded the remuda afoot so they could climb over the rock better.

Bill let them go on and did not follow until the remuda was around a bend and out of sight. He was leading Steeldust out of a pool when he heard a shot. Then he heard Pascual exulting with curses at the top of his voice. Bill led Steeldust into a tunnel that had been dug out by flood. He waited. He wished he had his pistol. He heard someone running and grunting toward him. A man came in sight and fell by the stream, exhausted. He was not one of the fleet young Indians who had taken the remuda. He carried a pistol in his hand. He was a tall, soft, heavy man, not used to running.

Pascual came in sight above him, grinning like a man would grin if he was trying to enjoy himself chewing nails. He ran lightly on the boulders over the head of his quarry. His pistol was in his belt.

The man stopped and looked over his shoulder at Pascual who laughed softly. The man whirled when he saw him, lost his balance and sat in shallow water on the edge of the stream. Pascual still had not drawn his pistol.

"Don't shoot me, Pascual," the man said in Spanish. "Please." He threw away his pistol.

"So it's you," Pascual replied. His smile was gone. The man panicked at his expression, jumped up and tried to get going in the sand again. Pascual jumped on his shoulders and drove his face into the shallow water. He picked the man's head up by the hair, twisted the face up close to his own and said, "Run, Anthrax. I like your form."

"I don't want to *run*, Pascual. I shouldn't have to run from you. I'm not your enemy."

"You're not a horse thief? You don't work for the Mexicans? Liar. You must be a General by now."

Bill stepped into the open. The man looked up at him as

though he were the Archangel Raphael. "Thank God, there he is," he said. "Look, Pascual, I was on my way to see this *gringo* about buying his horses when I met the Yaquis bringing them down the canyon. I have money to pay for the horses. Look in my pocket, Pascual."

Pascual ripped his clothes apart and lifted out his purse. He dropped the man's head in the water, opened the purse and spread gold coins out on the sand. He put them back in the purse and stowed it in his pocket.

"You never steal for your master, that one-armed freak, El Mocho Obregon?" Pascual asked. He gazed down at the man contentedly, benevolently. "You should have stayed in Mexico. Now, the Yaqui has caught you. Do you know how happy I am? Do you know what a great horse has brought me here today? My vengeance."

"Pascual, I'm only here to buy these horses. I didn't know they had been stolen. I didn't know you were here. As you know, I'm an officer of the forces of General Obregon. I buy his horses."

He stated this for Bill's benefit, hoping Bill understood Spanish, hoping to find mercy. Bill squatted and rolled a cigarette.

"I'm glad you steal," said Pascual. "Your vice gave you to me." He rolled the man over on his back and whacked the heel of his hand down against the man's large, bony nose.

"This is the Mexican we call La Carbonosa, The Anthrax," Pascual said to Bill. "He caused Yaquis more pain than a drought. He led the Cavalry in pursuit of the women and children at Vicam. He made a dashing figure at the head of the charge through our wives and little daughters. That must have made him feel brave enough to follow me here to see if he could take me for the reward." Pascual smashed the man's face with the heel of his hand, again.

"No, Pascual, no," squalled La Carbonosa. His face and voice were soggy with blood. "I'll make it up, Pascual. I'll do any penance. Don't disgrace my face."

"You are making it up."

"Listen, I'll give you the names of the Yaquis who helped me."

"I already know them. Didn't I just shoot one and watch the others run away without looking back for you? Didn't I ride down the canyon under their noses? I've known them all their lives. I knew their voices in the dark. After they followed me up here and found me for you and your money, did you think they would fight me, too?" Pascual stood up, disgusted. "Say their names, then. Who tracked me here? Weren't they the ones who built the bonfire on the rim?"

"The Mayos, Valenzuela and Moroyoqui."

"Which Moroyoqui? There are thousands."

"Alejandro. And the one you shot down here was a Yaqui, Marcos, in case you want to know that, too."

"True. You'll probably tell the truth now for the rest of your life."

"What else can I do? I know you are going to kill me. How could you let me live with my face like this?"

Pascual would not look at him.

"Punish me, kill me, but don't strike me in the face again, Pascual."

Bill climbed a boulder and counted the horses. "They're all here, Pascual," he said.

"The Anthrax had a chance to shoot me, but was too much a coward," said Pascual. "He doesn't know how to use his pistol when his target is looking him in the eye. This is the same disease who tied his neighbors' hands behind them, hobbled their feet, spat in their faces and hung them in front of their homes."

"No, Pascual," said La Carbonosa.

"Great Anthrax Fever, a Mexican germ."

"I had no reason to shoot you, Pascual. I'm not your enemy."

"We have to go back now, Bill," said Pascual.

Bill mounted Steeldust to start the horses back to camp.

He rode around a boulder and Steeldust almost jumped out from under him, shying at the Yaqui Pascual had killed. The boy was sitting with his dead eyes open and his back against the wall of the canyon where Pascual's shot had hurled him.

Pascual caught Joker, used one of Bill's reins for a bridle and mounted. He made La Carbonosa tie his oxfords together and hang them around his neck. La Carbonosa stood in his sock feet and smoked a cigarette.

"You'll walk more carefully to El Cedro in your socks," said Pascual. "I'll hang you there. I haven't brought my rope, or I'd do it here."

"Ask him to tell us who helps him steal horses in Arizona," Bill said. "Someone must have told him about these horses."

"You want the whole story?" asked La Carbonosa, pleading for Bill's attention. "The history? I am *authorized* by the Mexican and American Governments to buy horses here. The Mexican Government furnishes me money. I don't need to steal."

"Anthrax, walk," said Pascual softly, without looking at the man. "Herd these horses so Bill's great horse does not tire. Do one good thing before you die. Serve. Watch the flanks of the remuda, turn back horses who try to leave the canyon. Bill will bring his horse slowly behind you. Don't let Steeldust sweat. If he breaks a sweat, I'll cut off your ear. How would you like to go to God with your ears cut off and your nose split down the middle? You think you are worth anything anymore? Your disgraceful face is worth one drop of Steeldust's sweat."

"Pascual, I'll work. I know how to work," said La Carbonosa. He scrambled away after the remuda. Bill felt sorry for him. The remuda was easily contained by the walls of the canyon, but La Carbonosa ran his socks to shreds keeping the horses moving upstream. Pascual was riding in the lead. Bill held Steeldust to a walk so he would not sweat.

At El Cedro, Pascual corraled the horses, roped La Carbonosa around the neck and led him to the cottonwood where he had fed Steeldust the night before. A spring of clear water flowed out of the base of the cliff there. Pascual filled a tin cup with cool water and handed it to La Carbonosa.

"Have you anything to tell me?" asked Pascual.

"I've told you everything," said La Carbonosa. He held his cup with what he must have believed was elegance, extending his third and little fingers away, crooking them daintily. He handed the cup back to Pascual. "More, please, Pascual," he said. Pascual stooped to dip the cup in the spring again. La Carbonosa examined Bill while he waited for the drink. He seemed to feel secure, now, and no longer in need of help from Bill. Tom, Boots and Tony walked up to look at him. He probably felt Pascual would not hang him in front of *gringos*. His nose was no longer bleeding. He had come up the road to Calvary and found his reprieve under the tree.

"I didn't think your punishing my feet on the rocks was fair, Pascual," he scolded. "I won't complain about that now, but I wish to know what you will do with me."

"I'll be fair now," said Pascual.

"Thank God, Pascual," whispered La Carbonosa, bowing his head. "Thank you. I've always known you were a merciful man. That's why I was surprised you made me go barefoot on the rocks."

"More water?"

"No, Pascual, thank you."

"You want a drink of mescal?"

"Yes, Pascual. Everyone likes your mescal, myself included." La Carbonosa raised his voice and addressed Bill Shane and his crew. "This man famous, all Mexico, mescal." He turned to Pascual. "I don't know if your friends understand me."

Pascual filled the cup with mescal from a jug that lay cooling in the spring. "Anything more?" he asked gently as La Carbonosa drank.

"Maybe later I could eat."

"If you don't eat now, you won't eat."

"I've lost my appetite, Pascual. You're a hard man."

"I'm trying to be kind to you." Pascual lifted the oxfords gently from around La Carbonosa's neck, appraised them and handed them to him. The man sat down and put them on.

"Ah, my shoes are good on my feet." La Carbonosa sighed.

"We learned to herd goats barefoot, working together as boys for the Salido family. You began as an honest Mexican."

"Yes, Pascual, I did."

"That was the first step we learned in becoming men, how to work barefoot. We took no extra steps, wasted none."

"I understand, Pascual. I should not have tried to steal when I had the money for buying horses. I'm sorry. No harm done. Don't blame me for trying, Pascual." La Carbonosa winked at Bill and acted as though he was trying to hold a straight face.

"A thief *is* to blame. Do you want anything else?"

"Oh, no, Pascual, nothing, maybe just some shade, now."

"Shade you shall have," Pascual turned to Chapo, who had ridden up on a mule he had spent the morning tracking down. "Hoist this man into the tree by his neck and leave him until the sun goes down," Pascual ordered, handing Chapo the rope.

Chapo led La Carbonosa toward the cottonwood. La Carbonosa began weeping silently. He looked into the faces of the High Lonesome cowboys. He threw himself down once, but Chapo dragged him until he choked and clambered back to his feet. His voice resounded in the canyon when his breath came back, but he silenced himself and wept on quietly when Chapo stopped under the tree. Chapo threw the coils over a limb, caught the end of the rope, dallied on his saddlehorn, spurred his mule downhill, and hoisted La Carbonosa into the tree. La Carbonosa grabbed the rope above the honda to give himself slack, to no avail. He could not lift himself on the rope. The loop made a vice that was closing his head off from his body. He had to let go and strangle.

No one said a word. Pascual squatted in the shade of the tree, smoked and watched Steeldust. The horse watched the struggles of the man's body until it was still. Bill saw a tear fall from Pascual's eye as he watched the horse.

"That Mexican should have paid more than one death," Pascual said. "He killed families for money and when he could not catch them, he killed their livestock and burned their food. I grieve I cannot hang him again." He stood. "It turns out, he was too much disease to hang with one noose."

The cowboys were passing a cup of mescal in the shade. Pascual drank a swallow, held the cup for another and twirled La Carbonosa by his oxfords until he could see the face.

"He's dead enough, but we'll let him hang until sundown," Pascual said. "We'll bury him, but I would rather burn him like a carcass infected with the anthrax."

Chapo rode away with a pack mule and a tarp for the boy Pascual had shot in the canyon. Pascual drank from the cup again.

"One more swallow and no more for a while," he said.

"More for me. I want more," said Bill. He loved mescal with an inordinate love. He took the cup and drank again.

"It's no good," said Pascual. "I make it, but it's no good. Think of the great joy for life in a horse. He needs no mescal to make him feel joy, or passion, no spicy juices to make him feel more a horse. He enjoys his special moments in noble fashion and moves on. He swallows nothing to make him heady and foolish with his moments and no sins stain his days, or worry his nights. I always wanted to be a good man, worthy of a great horse. To my disgrace, on the day I was given to know the horse, I drank mescal all day and night and then killed two men."

Bill patted Pascual's shoulder and sipped the mescal. He looked into its clearness and anticipated the delight it was about to give him. Nothing could have made him put it down. He did not understand how anyone could think it was harmful.

"Don't feel bad, Pascual," Bill said. "You allowed the young ones to get away unharmed."

"I know their fathers and mothers, that's why. They're on their way back to Cajeme to farm corn now. The ones who had the fire on the rim are the bad ones. It's too bad those got away. I have been waiting for them. I knew if La Carbonosa ran into them on the desert he would contract them to betray me. I knew La Carbonosa would come after me this time. He followed me all my life, scraping at my leavings, looking to beat me to my goals. We've been rivals since we were boys. I hoped he would someday come to my canyon. It was time. All he needed was a Judas."

CHAPTER 7

A horse likes the warmth of another horse's side, the switch of a companion's tail on his face. He is happy in the goodness of other horses. He tries to remain unperturbed by man.

Turn him loose and watch and see who he seeks as a friend. Corral him, and the manner in which he is kept will show who is his enemy. Loan him promiscuously to anyone who comes along and watch how quickly he falls apart.

BILL, Tom, Pascual and the wranglers drove the remuda down to a deep, rocky ford on the Salt River. Rain showers had swelled the Salt off its droughty bed. The High Lonesome crew always crossed the horses where they had to swim because the cattle ford was dangerous with quicksand. A cow bogged in quicksand stopped and waited to be pulled out, but a horse in quicksand panicked and tore his joints apart.

The men ran the horses downhill so they hit the water running, plunged in and began to swim. Bill brought up the rear so Steeldust could watch and have a chance to figure what was expected of him. At the edge of the river, he picked fastidiously at his footing a moment, made his decision, and when Bill least expected it, launched himself over the water. His feet and legs flared out as he hit the water, and he sank like a skillet, taking Bill with him. He came up once and thrashed to swim, gave up, and sounded for bottom. Bill kicked loose to save himself. He hated to quit his horse in a storm, but after another drink like the first, Bill ruled that it was every man for himself.

Steeldust came up under Bill again and Bill felt the horse's head flinch away from his feet. He surfaced and Bill took hold of his mane and pointed him toward the other horses.

Bill was glad to hold on and float in close on Steeldust's downstream side. Bill's chaps, pistol and spurs were about to take him down for the third time and Bill had heard it said a man did not come up a third time. Steeldust was learning to swim, though. Horse and man were halfway across when the current whipped them and covered their heads again. The shock of that was so much Steeldust rolled over as though he was drowned, but his breath began to hurt him and he blew like a bellows and went on swimming. He found footing before Bill did and dragged Bill out to shallow water. He shook himself and nickered to the other horses.

Bill started laughing at the way he was blowing spray and blinking his eyes and turning them inside out. Steeldust turned back to Bill as if to say, "What the hell are you doing, laughing while you soak up more water, you want to drown?"

Bill sloshed out of the river and caught his horse. He led him in a circle while the water ran off them, then he mounted and rode after the other horses. A fine mist of rain caught up from the east on a cold breeze. Bill and Tom and the wranglers turned the remuda upstream and went on to help cross the herd.

The wagons crossed and Cap cooked a hot dinner at noon. The crew went in and changed clothes and caught fresh horses while the herd spread out and browsed in a sheltered draw.

That evening when Bill went to the fire for supper and another change of horses, he saw Steeldust was standing apart from the remuda with his head down, dozing.

"The feller's tired, this evening," Bill said. "He sounded for bottom today and that's different country than he ever saw before. It's hard coming back from those kind of new places."

Pascual laughed. "He tried to wing it across the Salt. He took such a leap, he almost made it."

"Did you see him sound for bottom? He made a suction like a toilet flushing and took me with him."

"He's no bird, that's certain," said Pascual. "He's more steel than feather, and steel doesn't float."

"I didn't expect him to float, but I didn't expect him to sound with his horseshoes, either."

"He had to find bottom. That's how he found out he would make it. He's made of steel dust."

From that day, Bill didn't say, "My colt," or "The little feller." He called him by name. Bill had been self-conscious about calling him Steeldust, because he felt naming him the same as the great horse sounded presumptuous to other cowboys, but after that day everybody started calling him Steeldust. Bill noticed even Lindano approved of the name.

The skies cleared and the sun went to work with a summer shine. The herd began to suffer in hot, still weather. One day, just before noon, Bill told Lindano to pass the word for the crew to rest the herd through the heat of the day. The herd was nearing shade and water where a stream ran through a stand of cottonwoods.

Lindano nodded and went on. He could not turn back a cow, or drive in the drags, but Bill thought he could be counted on to pass on an order that would enable him to stop in the shade for a while.

Bill was in the drags and saw the herd did not stop at the stream, but he could not do anything about it. He and Tom had to go after a bunch of cattle that spilled into a ravine. The heat and dampness was broiling their hats on their heads when they stopped the cattle in the bottom of the ravine. One old cow refused to leave the bottom. She backed up under a tree, shook her horns at Bill and laid down.

Bill dismounted, crawled under the tree, poked her in the ribs and tried to lift her by the tail. He might as well have been trying to uproot a tree. The water that ran off him could not have been all sweat, but it was the wrong color for blood, so Bill figured he was tapping some new reserve in his carcass. The stuff ran out of him as though he was being squeezed. He remounted and dropped the loop of a *reata* Pascual had given him over her horns and dragged her out from under the tree. Steeldust lunged, the *reata* slipped on the saddlehorn and blistered his hand. He thought, yeah, Pascual, that's why I carried that good manila, so I could give it away to you right when I needed it most.

Bill loosened the loop on the cow's horns; she rallied and started walking. Tom led the cow while Bill came behind her afoot, twisting her tail to keep her going and propping her up when she tried to go down.

The herd was making a big dust when Bill and Tom caught up. A big steer that had been with the leaders had fallen over dead in the heat. After supper, while everybody was by the fire, Bill reminded Lindano that he had been asked to tell the crew to rest the herd at noon.

"I misunderstood," Lindano said, looking away at the top of a tree.

"No, you didn't," Bill said, shaking his head.

"If you stopped this drive every time we came to a pretty stream, we'd never get to Red Rock. But no matter———"

"It matters. R.E. is now short one steer and he ought to be charged to you."

"And that matters *mucho*," said Cap and the whole crew laughed. Lindano went to his bedroll, lay down and turned his face to the brush.

Bill had been expecting the cattle to run since they forded the Salt. The herd was tired and hungry. The older steers would be the first to run. The old *ladinos* had not stampeded because the mother cows and calves made them feel responsible enough to stay in bounds. The cattle were being pushed through country that offered little forage. At night, the herd was too hungry to rest and too tired to eat. Even though the presence of mother cows and calves kept nervous cattle settled down, as the hardships of the drive increased, so did the likelihood that some start or fright would make everybody run.

On the morning after the big steer died, the herd was on its feet long before first light. Jonas roused the crew earlier than usual. Bill saddled Steeldust and hurried to the lead as the leaders lined out, looking for a better place. The wranglers pointed the remuda out ahead of the cattle. The herd climbed to a saddle and started down a steep trail by a canyon.

The trail led into a corner of a fence and made a ninety-degree turn along the fence. The cattle crowded against the fence on the turn. The fence was on the outside of the turn, uphill from the trail. A cliff bordered the trail on the inside of the turn. The scare of the 100-foot drop off the cliff kept the herd crowded against the fence. Cattle walking by the cliff edge leaned sharply inboard as they shoved their way along the brink.

Bill was riding between the remuda and the leaders of the cattle. Tony and Lindano were riding beside him. Boots Vail was ahead of the horses. Lindano chose that moment to school Little Pie. Little Pie had his mind on the horses as he started off the mountain. The remuda was trying to hurry. Little Pie was prancing to keep up. Lindano could not keep him still so he decided to teach him to back up. He began pulling on Little Pie to back him up. Instead of telling him to "Back," he pursed his lips and made a kissing sound, a signal for any horse to go forward. He spurred the horse, another signal for him to go forward. The horse wanted to go forward. Everybody but Lindano was trying to go forward. Little Pie could not understand Lindano's intent so he began to rear up. Lindano cursed and spurred him to punish him.

"How can the horse go on when you keep pulling him to go back?" Bill asked Lindano.

"Back is where I want him to go," said Lindano through clenched teeth.

"But everybody else is going forward. The whole drive is headed down this trail to Red Rock."

"He knows what I want him to do. He'll back up, because I've taught him to go back when I want him to."

Little Pie threw his head down, shook it in frustration and floundered toward the edge of the cliff. The leaders stopped and held back cattle that were trying to get by the cliff. The leaders were watching Little Pie and looking for safe country. Cattle swelled toward the edge of the cliff. Jake Breach's spotted oxen began prowling along behind Steeldust as though they were armored and would not be stopped. Then Bill heard a rumble of hooves and bodies as cattle flushed by the cliff. Wire burst and staples whined off posts on the fence. In another instant the herd would flatten the fence and scatter over the mountain, spill off the cliff, or carry Bill and his partners off the mountain on their horns. Tony raised his hand and shouted at the leaders. A big, black steer went head and heels over the fence.

"Give 'em room. Let 'em go," Bill shouted and slapped Tony's mule on the hips with the coils of his *reata* and drove him after the remuda. The remuda was already chasing Boots off the mountain. Lindano gave Little Pie his head to save himself and Little Pie scrambled to run under the man's weight with his eyes big and scared. Then the three men sold out any lease they had on life while they outran the stampede off the mountain.

At the bottom, the herd dropped into a wide, sandy wash and spread out along the banks. Tom appeared ahead of the remuda to help Boots. Only a third of the cattle had come on with the leaders. Cattle were scattered all over the mountain. Many had turned and run back over the saddle, away from the scare at the cliff. Cowboys and horses were taking chances to contain the herd. The leaders slowed in the sand, their heads down and their eyes cooling. Bill and Tony watched Lindano keep right on going, just flying and quirting his horse and not looking back for the spooks. Bill laughed at him. Bill had been in many a stampede and always expected trouble when he drove past that turn in the trail to Red Rock, but he did not think he had ever been in one in which the phalanx boogered his heels like this one.

Lindano came back after a while and shouted, "Now, hold that bunch, if you can, while I see about gathering the rest of the herd. Don't *ever* let cattle run like that again."

Bill laughed again and this time Tony gave him a dirty look. Bill knew Tony was still smarting because he had started the kid's mule off the mountain with the coil of his *reata*. Bill thought, Hell, a cowboy doesn't figure to stop three thousand cattle by waving his hand at them when he's standing in their downhill bog. A kid's dirty looks were not going to make Bill feel bad. He was too happy he and his horse were still alive and still held the leaders.

"There ain't a geezer on this drive whose biscuits is done," said Tony, trying to sound cowboy. Lindano wheeled his horse and dashed away with more orders on his breath. The leaders were quiet and since Tom was nearby, Bill rode after Lindano.

Bill wanted to keep watch on Lindano until the herd was back together. The last time Lindano had been with Bill on a stampede, he had run off a bunch of cattle and then gone back and sold them.

That evening the crew pointed the herd down the main street of Sunrise, Arizona. The street led through the town to a large dam that held a lake of clear water.

Bill was riding Joker and he stationed himself in the end of the street to hold the cattle on the water. A big brindle steer filled himself with water and strolled by to see what he could see. The steer was tall as Joker. He ambled onto a boardwalk in front of a vacant store. He caught sight of himself mirrored in the window and backed up so fast his hind end fell off the walk. He caught himself and gathered for combat. He wrung his tail and spurted manure straight out behind him and bawled and glared at himself, recognizing an awful beast. He bellowed as though he was standing over a dead carcass. He shook his horns and armed himself for the devil.

He glared at himself and his image did not look away. He glanced away for avenues of escape while he kept one eye on himself. He moved forward and the tip of one horn rapped on the glass. He jerked his head around and rapped the glass with the other horn. He backed slowly, pawed the walk, whipped and curled his tail, bellowed and pressed his forehead down against the walk. He straightened and looked around to see if anybody else was aware of this new beast he had discovered. He advanced to the window and touched his nose gingerly to the glass, flinched, shook his horns and put his wet muzzle to the glass again. His nostrils cringed.

He must have decided then that he enjoyed the sight of himself, for he began to admire himself. He moved his head from side to side, so he could look at himself out of one eye and then the other. He raised his head and looked down his nose at himself, finally saw enough, lowed softly and walked away.

Bill began helping move the herd off the water. He looked down the street for more help. He saw Lindano ride into the street on a brown horse called Mike from Bill's mount of horses. A man was looking for a fight when he mounted a horse from another cowboy's string. Any time a foreman caught a horse out of a cowboy's string and gave him to someone else to ride, he was indicating he had just fired the cowboy. Lindano could not fire Bill so he must be asking for a fight. And Bill was ready to give him one. He had a lot of respect for that Mike horse.

Lindano began making Mike prance in front of a cantina to music from a gramophone. He worried the horse with his spurs while he held him back and made him arch his neck.

Tom followed Bill up the street to back him up. Tony was

drinking with a crowd in front of the cantina. Bill stopped between the crowd and Lindano. Lindano had a glaze on his eye while he tortured Bill's horse to the tune of the music.

"Pull up," Bill said.

Lindano's face was sweating. "Watch this, watch this, watch this," he said and kept right on lathering the horse.

"Get off him," Bill said.

"It's all right, all right. Watch me," Lindano said. He hooked his reins over the saddlehorn and rode with both hands on his hips.

Bill reached over and picked the reins off the horn, stripped the bridle off Mike. Tom stung Mike with his quirt and Lindano's eyes lost their glaze as the horse almost jumped out from under him.

Lindano lost both stirrups as Mike lunged away, but he stayed on by squeezing the horn with both hands and hugging the swells of his saddle with his knees. Mike raced down the street toward a bunch of horses tied to a tree. Mike slammed into the horses and they broke loose and scattered out of town with him. Mike stuck his head into the first stand of brush outside town at a dead run. Lindano came out on the other side with no hat and only half his shirt. Mike headed for another stand of brush. Lindano decided he had enough of that, turned loose all holds, kicked both feet up, rolled off Mike's hips and bounced his face on the ground.

Mike shied and veered off and came nickering back toward town. Boots rode up and caught him against a building and led him back toward Bill. Bill guessed Boots figured Lindano would be heading back to Bill, too.

Lindano picked himself up and went back into the brush for his hat. He was carrying his quirt on his left wrist, whipping his leg with it and walking as straight as he could toward Bill. Boots began telling Bill he had tried to stop Lindano from catching Mike out of the remuda. Lindano came on and stopped down the street, out of range for fists, just in range for a pistol.

"Nobody snatches my bridle," said he.

"What's the matter, wasn't fun?" asked Bill.

Lindano pulled Tony's pistol out of his chaps, playing for the crowd. "These people came to watch a horse dance, Shane. You didn't like the way the brown danced? Let's see how yours dances." He fired a round past Bill's head.

Joker was not gun-shy. He threw his head up, but he stood for it. Lindano fired another round by Bill's head and then sighted the pistol at Bill's face.

"Want some fun, Shane? Start laughing."

"Shoot again, but if you miss me, I'm going to make you eat the pistol," Bill said.

Lindano stiffened his arm like a target shooter, lowered the muzzle and lined it up on Bill's breast bone. He wanted it known he was ready to shoot a man, but he was grinning and his face showed he knew his hand was doing something he should not be letting it do. Bill did not mind looking at the pistol as long as that grin was behind it.

"Don't be afraid, Shane. I'll let you go, this time," Lindano said. "This time the joke was on me." He quit looking down his sights at Bill and glanced around to make sure the crowd was watching him. Bill found Tony in the crowd.

"See the pistol, kid?" asked Bill.

Tony and everybody else was looking at the weapon at that moment.

"Recognize the piece?"

"Why should I?" asked Tony.

"Is it yours?"

Lindano kept grinning and put the pistol away in his chaps. "I carry no weapon but my own," he said. He turned away and started walking.

"If that's my gun, I want it back," said Tony.

Lindano laughed and walked through the crowd to the cantina.

"He wouldn't be carrying my gun," Tony said. "What's

the matter with you? He has a gun of his own just like it. He wasn't bothering you. That horse could have killed him."

"He was killing the horse. He can have his parties afoot. He were partying with my horse and my horses are not to be used for entertainment of any kind. You and your daddy's pet ape can ride mules when you want to party."

"You don't have the right to put any man in that kind of danger."

"If you want to get drunk with Lindano and show off when you ought to be working, that's your business. It's my business to keep apes and drunks off my horses. I'm better at my business than you are at yours. Think about that when you go to your daddy to draw your wages."

"Don't lecture me. I'm a man. You don't tell me how to behave."

"You're no man, Baby Fat."

Tony turned and followed Lindano into the cantina.

The next afternoon Bill caught up to Tony working the drags. He was supposed to be helping Boots or Cap, but Bill figured since he was no real help to them, he might as well be in the drags. Bill might even have left him alone, but he was roping the heels of tired cattle. Tony had seen Bill coming, roped the heels of an old cow, rode off, and dragged the cow to show off.

"I'll be the best heeler in Arizona if I can get down here to rope every day," he bragged, looking over his shoulder at Bill.

"Then learn when not to rope," Bill said. "These cattle are tired and they still have a long way to go."

"Everybody does it."

"It's wrong, so put up your rope."

"I will, because my arm is getting sore, but you don't stop me from roping my own cattle."

"Where did you get the idea they were your cattle?"

"If they aren't mine now, they soon will be."

"That must be why your daddy sent you on this drive, so

you could rope your cattle and look after your pistol. You haven't had time for anything else, have you?"

Bill laughed and rode away. He was getting just about enough of Tony. He guessed Tony did not think much of him, either. The slow dust and manure of the drags was just right for Tony, as far as Bill was concerned, if he could be kept from roping the cattle.

Juan Charro was another one Bill had to watch. He was supposed to help on the herd now and then, after the wagons had been moved and were in place for Cap. Bill noticed the wider the cattle strayed on the flanks of the drive, the wider Juan Charro strayed. If the cattle went into the brush for shade, he just rode wider and let them have more brush. He never turned them back so they would keep walking.

Bill happened to be watching one day when Juan Charro rode around a thicket and disappeared. Bill rode to the wagon later and found him squatting on his haunches with coffee and a biscuit and talking with Cap. Cap would put up with anybody for a chance to talk. That day Juan Charro had made five trips to the wagon for coffee and biscuits.

The herd was on good feed that day and the crew rode hard to keep it moving. Tom, Pascual and Bill were so busy they did not have time to stop for dinner. They changed horses three times that day. By evening Juan Charro had not changed horses, the horse he rode all day was not tired, and Juan Charro was not hungry.

Bill was counting the herd through a gate into a fenced pasture for the night when Juan Charro rode up, belched and said, "I'm going to the wagon."

"What for? Can't stay away?" Bill asked.

Juan Charro blinked and belched again. "I'm sick."

"How sick?"

"Bad sick."

"What's wrong?"

"I don't know, it's my chest, my belly. Maybe gas."

"Too many beans."

"Something."

"What're you going to the wagon for? The wagon's your trouble."

"Cap's got soda. Anybody here got soda?"

After supper, Tom, Pascual and Bill were catching horses to ride the pasture fences and to see the cattle were watering. Lindano came up and ordered Pascual to take charge of the remuda. Pascual, according to Lindano's calculations, knew the country best and would keep the remuda on good pasture. Pascual was too good a cowboy to be leaving the herd to wrangle horses, but he was not making opposition to the order. Bill saw him look relieved at the prospect of an easier job. That day they all would have jumped at an easier job. Lindano had no authority to change Pascual's job, but Bill could see he would rather wrangle and Bill was too worn out to have a fight over authority with Lindano that day.

"Tony's no good on the remuda," said Lindano. "He's my responsibility so I'm putting him on the herd where he can learn more about cattle. Pascual will make sure all the horses work. Some of these cowboys are riding their gentle horses to death while their bronc horses are fattening up. Jonas is the only man on the crew with enough guts to ride his broncs."

Grounding Tony in the drags seemed like a fine idea so Bill and Tom rode off and left Pascual to wrangle. Neither said anything for a while. Bill was quiet because he was beginning to realize Tom and he would be working twice as hard with the herd without Pascual.

"Why'd you let that monkey take Pascual away from us?" asked Tom. "Now we've got a whelp in the drags to look after instead of a man to help us."

"That's been worrying me, too. Tony in the drags and Pascual with the remuda is just like five good men rode away to town," Bill said.

"One thing about it, when the sweat is splashing off you

and you find Tony laying in the shade, just remember you've made your friend Pascual comfortable, too. That's what I call a good friend. A dumb son of a gun who'll be sure his best hand is twiddling his thumbs watching the horses graze while everybody else is working."

After supper, Bill took a chance and went looking for Juan Charro. He found him taking his coffee and biscuits with Cap and Pascual behind the chuckwagon. Cap was telling them a story. Pascual was whittling on a stick.

"Juan Charro, you've got a new job," Bill announced. "Lindano says you're nighthawk from now on. He wants the wrangling all done right. Tony's taking your place as swamper and rider of the drags."

Pascual's chest swelled with a sigh, but he kept on whittling with his head down. Bill wanted to see what he would say about having to go back to work, but he just kept on whittling. He had known all along where he belonged.

"That's just right," said Juan Charro. "I'm bored."

"You won't be bored with the nighthawk," said Bill. He began to laugh because Pascual gave him a blank look and went on whittling. Pascual would be coming back to the herd against his will, but he knew he had to do right. Bill kept on laughing because he could see Pascual had been counting on resting his bones beside the horses. Pascual stood up, sheathed his big knife and went to his saddle and blankets. He needed to sleep now if he was to make a hand on the herd.

Bill followed him and sat under a tree near him. He began to laugh again, proud of himself. Tony was in the drags where he most belonged, Juan Charro doing night work, and Pascual was back with the herd without ever having been gone.

"You enjoy depriving a sore, overworked man of his rest, don't you, white man?" said Pascual.

"Better you and me doing my work than just me," Bill said.

"You could not stand to see me enjoy some comfort."

"Why should you be comfortable?"

"Ah, you'll see."

Juan Charro brought in the remuda and roused the crew two hours before dawn the next day. Bill decided he had better have a talk with Juan Charro so he would know not to awaken the crew an hour too early the next day. Pascual offered to catch the horses for Tom. Tom seemed glad to let Pascual show his hand at roping horses in the dark. Bill came up late and asked for Steeldust. Pascual could not find him so he caught Mike. Mike was darker and harder to find, but neither man could see Steeldust. They knew he was there. They had both seen him when Juan Charro brought in the remuda.

Bill, Tom, Pascual and Tony rode together around the herd to start it off the bedground in the dark. Pascual lit a match for a cigarette and Tony took it from his hand and held it close to his mount's ear and quickly shook it out. Bill saw he was riding a horse, not a mule. Pascual asked him why he was looking at his horse's ears.

"What do you need to see?" asked Pascual.

Tony lit another match. "This is not my horse, either," he said quietly. "This animal is trying to buck me off and pile my head on a rock in the dark. This is Steeldust."

Bill woke up. Pascual laughed. "You suppose I caught you a horse instead of a mule? How could anybody make such a mistake?"

"Did you give this kid my horse, Pascual?" Bill asked. He rode up beside Tony to look at the animal in the dark. He could not recognize one detail of his own horse.

"Can you imagine a mistake like that, Bill? I must be getting old, or I'm not getting enough rest. Better look and be sure. I know how you hate for anybody else to ride your top horse. I know how it spoils him."

Just then the horse hunched and swelled, gathered his

butt and boogered away. "Whoa, boy—whoa, boy—whoa," coaxed Tony. The horse froze because he could not see well enough to buck.

"He's going to do it to me again," said Tony. "And I don't know how to stop him."

Bill struck a match and recognized his horse.

"This man on his high horse next to you knows what to do. Ask him," said Pascual.

"Get off, Baby Fat," Bill said. He dismounted and unsaddled Mike. Tony was not moving an eyelash.

"Get off," Bill said and held Steeldust's rein for him. Pascual and Tom laughed and rode on.

"What's the matter, Shane?" Tom called back. "Was the kid violatin' your baby? Maybe you're the only one knows the horse from a mule."

Tony dismounted and Bill unsaddled Steeldust for him while he walked around to steady his legs which were shaking from fright. Bill saddled Steeldust and waited for Tony to saddle Mike. The kid fumbled and cursed so long Bill was sure he would still be afoot when the sun came up and the cattle stood up on the bedground. Bill did not blame him for not knowing a horse from a mule in the dark. Pascual had fooled them both. However, Bill knew he was full of Tony because he wanted to ride off and leave him. He had better manners than to ride away while a cowboy was trying to saddle a horse, but it sure tried his patience to wait. Tony did not appreciate his good manners, either. He finally saddled and mounted and rode away from Bill, mumbling to himself.

Steeldust kept trying to buck all morning and every time he humped up, it seemed Tom was watching. "Oh, oh, Baby's going to do it to his Daddy," Tom would yell. "Baby's got the ringtail today."

Bill did not change horses at noon so he could ride the lumps out of Steeldust. He rode by the drags that afternoon and found Tony bare to the waist, sunning himself horseback. He was shadowriding along, knotting his muscles and watching them bulge on his shadow on the ground. Bill rode behind him awhile to see what else he would do. Tony took off his hat so the sun could touch his brow. Once in a while he waved his hat at the cattle like a dude. Often he had complained around camp that he was getting a white forehead and a burned face. This was unsightly for a member of a family of his stature—bankers and salamanders. Salamanders just loved the sun when they had plenty of shade nearby.

Tony was so busy shadowriding he rode into the herd and cut back two oxen. The oxen walked into a thicket and stopped with their heads together. Tony stopped outside the thicket and yelled at them and waved his hairless hand at them to scare them out.

He turned to Bill, looking helpless as a frog stung by a scorpion, and said, "I can't go in there. Would you please bring those idiot oxen out?"

Bill just looked at him.

"I can't ride in that brush. I went up for coffee and left my shirt at the wagon."

"You need an extra hand to ride along to keep you from being scratched in the brush?" Bill asked. "What are you good for?"

Bill rode into the thicket. Tony rode after the drags, confident Bill would do his job. "Thank you," he called back.

Bill started one old ox out and the other circled in the thicket behind him. He went back to the second ox and the first stuck his head in the brush again. He dismounted with his rope and beat on their horns to drive them out. The sweat was rolling off him when he remounted and he was cranky, but the oxen had taught him not to ride along spying on Tony Claire.

Bill rode to the wagon. He wanted that shirt for the rest of the day. He found it close to the wagon on the ground.

He stuffed it in a morral he carried on his saddlehorn. Cap saw him pick it up.

Bill kept the herd between himself and Tony through the afternoon. Everytime he saw Tony the boy was hotter and redder from the sun. After Tony knew he was suffering too much sun it was harder for Bill to keep the herd between them.

Bill was busy toward the end of the day and forgot about Tony until the boy rode up shouting Bill's name. Cap must have told him Bill had his shirt. He was on fire, but Bill hated for anyone to call his name out loud.

"You stole my shirt, Bill Shane," Tony shouted, catching Steeldust's rein.

"I found your shirt," Bill said. "Say thank you."

"You let me get sunburned. You stole it just to watch me burn, like you stole my pistol." He slapped Bill's leg. This did not satisfy him so he slapped Steeldust on the side of the head with his hat.

Bill was holding a piggin' string in his hand, a length of braided manila. He was always practicing tying one handed knots in it to mark hundreds in a herd when he was counting.

"You already found your pistol," Bill said.

"Where's my shirt? Give it to me." Tony reached for the morral on Bill's saddlehorn. Bill pushed his hand away. Tony slapped Steeldust with his hat again. Bill brought the knotted cord down on his forehead and put the marks of three knots on his scowl. Tony sailed his hat away and grabbed Bill's shirt and tried to pull him off his horse. Bill turned Steeldust's shoulder into his horse and he let go. Bill picked up the loop of his *reata* in his hitting hand.

"Don't try again, Baby Fat," Bill said. "I'll knock down your ear."

"Get off your horse. You're going to fight me man to man." Tony's chin was trembling. "I've been the butt of your jokes and ridicule since the day this drive began and you're going to quit it. Get off your horse."

"I'm off," Bill said and dismounted. Steeldust dropped his head and rested. Bill slapped him on the rump to get him out of the way, but he just raised his head, then put it back down to graze.

"Come on and fight," said Tony, raising his fists.

Bill stepped toward him and his feet ran off three paces with him. Bill stepped up again and he charged with his head down. Bill stepped aside and hooked him in his baby fat as he went by. Tony's own weight put him down on his face. He was not good at taking his knocks. He stayed on the ground while Bill mounted, dropped his shirt on him and went back to work.

The rest of the day Tony roamed around the herd bareheaded with little purpose except to keep up with the crew so he could be present at suppertime. Bill rode back for his hat and carried it to the wagon.

Tony came late for supper. His lip was still down. He rode Mike right up to the fire and tied him near the dutch ovens that were holding Cap's supper. He was already in so much trouble that Cap did not scold him. He filled his plate with food, left the lid off the biscuits and sat down on his bedroll. Mike backed up, raised his tail and dropped manure on Cap's sourdough biscuits. Cap raised up from his cooking and watched him and said nothing.

Tony threw down his plate and ran at the horse. "You stupid horse," shouted he. "Worthless, stupid horse." Mike danced away from him and kicked dirt and manure into the bean-pot. Tony grabbed his reins and kicked Mike in the belly. Cap looked down at his ruined biscuits, picked a clean skillet off the chuckwagon and started after Tony. Tony was twelve inches taller than he was.

"You're the idiot. The horse didn't tie himself next to my fire," Cap said.

"The damned idiot needs a good beating," shouted Tony. He was not paying enough attention to Cap. Right then he should have been remembering the clean job of castigation

Cap had performed on him the last time he was sloppy in camp. Tony stooped to pick up a stick. Mike backed into the wagon, knocked over the chuck box and danced over Cap's steaks and peeled potatoes. Cap dropped his skillet on Tony's head. Tony went down on his face again, twitched and raised dust with the toes of his boots. The whole crew walked away to find something else to do while Tony woke up crying again.

The crew let the boy completely alone for a week. He grew leaner. He began mounting his mules in a smoother manner. He quit complaining. Every now and then he showed up in the right place at the right time, like a cowboy. He began earning his wages. He did not seem to hold a grudge after the herd crossed the Gila. Pascual loaned him some of his horses and Tony learned that cowboying could have its rewards just in the correct use of a good horse. He watched Bill at work and often went along and backed him up. Bill was glad to see him coming, sometimes. He knew the boy would someday be a banker, but he found himself overlooking that.

CHAPTER 8

To know your horse's humor, look to your own strange pursuits.

HIGH winds from the southwest boiled dust into a tower above the herd as it started across the last 50 miles of desert to Red Rock. Cap's camp was bare and the desert afforded no protection against the storm. Cattle bedded down at night with their tails to the wind. Riders hunched their shoulders, horses clamped their tails against the storm. Beds, hats, and clothing were made abrasive by the dust. The cook's fire was subdued and cool. Cap's chuck was cold. His biscuits made the sound of the sandstorm inside a cowboy's head when he chewed.

The cattle fought for room and spread out as they left the Gila. Riders were obscured by the storm and the cattle wandered wide. The crew began allowing the weaker cows and calves to drop back. The cattle were close enough to Red Rock to be gathered after the weather cleared.

The work doubled. The tired and dispirited cattle were balking. The most spirited, the bunch quitters, watched for every opportunity to break away.

The storm began to win its hold. Desert, men and animals gave way to the wind. The world wore red dust. Bill watched Lindano. He knew Lindano always had mischief in mind.

The path of the herd became so broad that it was a half mile ride from one side to the other—the crew changed horses four times a day.

The height of the storm came the second day after the herd left the Gila. Bill watched Lindano ride after six big steers. Tom had just turned them into the herd, but as soon as his back was turned, they veered out again and headed for home.

Lindano rode wide as though he wanted to turn them back. He was hunched down under his woolen poncho, his hat crammed nearly to his collar. The dust was so thick and stung so much a man seldom looked up for another cowboy. Bill lagged and let Lindano go on. Lindano glanced once over his shoulder like a coyote looking to see if the coast was clear so he could squat and leave a mess. Bill stayed back and watched him ride into the storm. After a while, he followed. Lindano's tracks showed he had gone with the steers straight away from the herd.

Later, Bill squatted with Cap, Jonas and the Breach brothers in the lee of the wagon with hot coffee, biscuits and Karo syrup. Bill held one of Cap's soft, white biscuits in his black and knotted hand while Cap poured Karo syrup, clear as a jewel, on the biscuit.

"Boy, that's nice, Cap," Bill said. "Syrup and biscuits might keep us from blowing away."

"Have some more. Have another biscuit, but be quick. I want to hide the Karo before Pascual sees it. He drinks it by the cupful. Drinks it straight."

Bill looked at the faces of Jonas and the Breach brothers. The Breaches were blond and blue-eyed. Jonas was red-headed and freckled. Jonas never tanned. He burned to a spotted veneer that peeled and fell off his face in pieces and left scabs beside patches of delicate white. The Breach brothers' lips were blistered, cracked and bleeding. Their red eyes rolled inside a crust of dust and tears. Bill knew he would be doing these three men a favor by letting them drop back with the stragglers and bunch quitters. They could ride with their backs to the wind for a while.

"If you three fellers will do us a favor and keep the

stragglers from drifting too far, we'll have them when the wind stops," Bill said. "You'll need to locate the big, active quitters and throw them in with the cows."

The three cowboys wore the same look of veteran cowhorses who had just been ridden hard and put away wet. All three groaned involuntarily because they were being caught and saddled for a new job before they had been given a chance to rest from the old one.

"I'm asking you three to do it because you're the best men for it," Bill said.

"I'll go, Honey," said Jonas. "I'm riding a bad tasting son of a gun who needs sweetening with extra work in a windstorm. I had him going good before the sandstorm began peppering his ass."

"Me and Jake will go," said Alex.

"Who's going to look after our cattle?" asked Jake.

"Jake, don't be an old woman," said Alex.

"I'm serious. I'm on this drive to see my own cattle to market. I don't need to say goodbye to my cattle and go off where something might happen to me. I might not be enough cowboy to keep weak cattle and juicy cattle together in a windstorm. When I'm home where I belong I'm just a storekeeper."

"You've always been a better cowboy than a storekeeper," said Alex. "Look at it this way, cattle are more fun to keep on the shelf."

"Make up your mind, Jake," said Bill. "You can stay with the herd if you want."

"He'll go," said Alex.

"Wait a minute, what are we up against?" asked Jake. "I know the kind of country we're in. I know this trail, too. Listen, I'm no tough and I'm sure no fighter."

"I'll tell you right now," said Bill. "I just saw Lindano drive six head off the flank and two of them belonged to you. So you'll see some of your own cattle back there."

"Listen, Jake, we all know what Lindano would like to

do," said Alex. "The place for us is back where we can catch the cattle he shaves off the herd."

"You'll be riding hell out of your horses," Bill said. "Try to hold the cattle on the Gila. Ride the line of the river bed and hold on that line.

"The Yaquis in this country know we're here with a herd of beef. They're hungry and they can use the storm to gather meat and hides. They won't fight, but don't risk your hides to protect cattle. I'd rather they didn't drive cattle off in bunches, but let 'em do it if they want to. They'll leave tracks. We'll bring back all the cattle they haven't eaten after the storm. If you catch Yaquis butchering a steer, stay on your horses and ride away to show you don't care. While they're butchering and eating, they can't be stealing bunches.

"We're only two weeks drive from Red Rock, but if the storms keeps up the herd will turn and run. Then we'll all join you on the Gila. Don't take any wild rides and don't get down off your horse afoot. Keep your backs to the wind and you'll have a better chance of keeping track of your cattle. Try to face them back into the storm and you got troubles."

"I'll catch our horses," said Jonas. The meeting broke up.

Later, Bill saw Jonas and the Breach brothers leaving downwind and taking cattle. Jake was leading five horses in a string tied head to tail. Two of the horses were packed with beds and provision. The other three constituted the remuda.

Lindano was nearby. He turned his head to look at Bill and saw the cowboys riding downwind. His eyes were slitted against the storm and he could not hide his hate for Bill.

"Jonas and the Breach brothers are staying back," Bill said.

"What's the matter, losing cattle?" Lindano asked. "In this little storm?"

"I notice you head downwind quite a bit yourself, in the little storm. One by one these cattle have been turning around and heading home, or haven't you noticed?"

"Oh, I haven't noticed."

Jonas had been out with the Breach brothers twenty-four hours. The dust of the main herd did not seem to be advancing, but the cattle Jonas and the Breaches were handling were trying to leave the country on the wind. Jake led the horses with the main body of cattle. Jonas and Alex rode on his flanks and threw cattle to him.

Jonas rode to a hill to investigate a cloud of dust. He hid himself as much as he could. He wanted to see cattle before they saw him so he could ride to the front of them and stop them. The sight of him would scare the bunch quitters into a trot and make them hard to overtake.

He stopped on the hill as soon as he could see over the top of it. Lindano was on the other side driving eleven big steers across a flat. Jonas made his horse stand still. He heard a shout on the wind and Lindano's horse stopped. The cattle stopped. Lindano's poncho flapped and Little Pie's mane and tail sprayed in the wind. Lindano rode to the top of another hill and seemed to address some rocks.

Jonas considered the trouble. He was riding a four-year-old bronc he called Copper. Copper was deep chested, hog backed and entertained in his breast the disposition of a rabid javalina. He was the kind who would do anything to rid himself of his rider and he even had the power to levitate when he wanted to do it. He was not a fair-minded horse. He was dirty and superhuman. If he could not hurt Jonas with honest bucking, he became subhuman and tried to commit suicide or maim himself, anything so that he could have Jonas at a disadvantage. Copper would not be Jonas' ally in any argument with Lindano.

Then, one of the rocks in front of Lindano straightened into a tall Indian who walked a step, picked something off the ground and squatted again.

There, now, another card has fallen, thought Jonas. Here's the deal. Lindano, a thief, has run into somebody hungry who probably also wants to steal. I'm riding a criminal who wants my gizzard and I'm threatened by armed thieves who want my cattle. The cattle are the type who would rather hook me with a horn or run over me than allow me to take charge of them. I find myself wide awake and without a friend in Arizona.

Lindano was riding back toward the herd and leaving the cattle. Six Yaquis stood up and disappeared off the hill. Copper began to dance and fidget. Jonas rode him into a wash and worked him in the sand to take the edge off him. He rode back up the hill and saw the Indians walking in the open toward the cattle. The cattle lined out to leave the country. The Yaquis spread out and got ahead of them and held them in a stand of *palo verde* trees.

Jonas knew he could go back to the Breach brothers and not say anything about seeing these cattle, and the Yaquis would take them and nobody but Lindano would know. Jonas' skin would not get scratched that way. He would be obeying Bill's orders. He decided instead to let the Yaquis know that HL cattle came with cowboys. If Yaquis wanted cattle they would have to leave Jonas afoot to take them. He quit hiding. He rode out so the Yaquis could have a good look at him. He saw he had only six Yaquis. They kept their places around the cattle and watched Jonas ride toward them.

The tallest Yaqui walked out to meet him when he was close enough to talk. The Indian watched Copper and ignored Jonas. He knew Copper was a bronc. Old Copper was pure Yaqui that day. He was bound to take sides with Jonas' enemy, whether his enemy be a barbwire fence, a brushy tree, a cliff or a cow thief.

As he neared the Indian, Copper began to swell with meanness. He let his eyes start in his head, pretending the Yaqui was a haunt. This was not an involuntary bugging of the eyes. Copper was pretending the Yaqui horrified him and Jonas was doing wrong making him walk up close to him. He caught his first smell of the Yaqui and he sashayed sideways from him. Jonas brought him back and made him walk closer to the Yaqui. Copper raised his head and snorted at the Indian, trying Jonas' patience in front of his adversaries.

"*Buenas tardes,*" said Jonas in Spanish. "You honey of a gut-eatin' heathen," said he under his breath in English.

The Yaqui examined Copper, ignoring Jonas. "*Buenas,*" he said. He stepped behind Copper and lifted his tail. Copper trembled, turned back, and snorted at the Yaqui.

"Thank you for gathering our strays," Jonas said in Spanish.

"Are you a Mexican?" the Yaqui asked in English.

"I'm Texan, a cowboy for the *Alto Y Solo,* the High Lonesome herd. Thank you for holding our cattle. These cattle strayed from the herd that raises yonder dust."

"Your cattle? These are Yaqui cattle, for us to eat. All brushy flat—north, south and west of the Gila—depends on the Yaqui. All these trails are Yaqui. This sorrel you are riding is also Yaqui."

"No, this stock belongs to Bradford, the Redhead. It depends on Matus, his *caporal.*"

"You are the Redhead's son?"

"Only one of his many cowboys."

"Matus is nobody's man."

"Matus is helping the Redhead."

"Where is Matus?"

"There, with the dust of the herd."

"When will you see our friend Matus?"

"At suppertime."

"I am Moroyoqui, the Mayo. Cousin of Matus."

"Help me back with these cattle and we'll eat meat and drink coffee with Matus."

"I do not wish to see Matus."

"So you are the Mayo, Moroyoqui."

"*Egui,* yes."

"Pascual has mentioned you. You visit him in Cedar Canyon."

Jonas rode by Moroyoqui and stood Copper among the cattle. Moroyoqui broke off a long, supple branch of chaparral and came up behind him. The switch set Copper to dancing. Jonas knew it was time to take a deep seat. He started moving the cattle. The Yaquis turned the cattle back. Moroyoqui stung Copper on the thigh with the switch. Copper kicked and Jonas spun him to face the Indian.

"Go on to your supper with Matus," said Moroyoqui.

"I'm taking the cattle," said Jonas. "I'm armed."

Moroyoqui waved the switch under Copper's nose. Copper snorted, shied and threw himself backward into the cattle. "So am I," said Moroyoqui. He drew his machete. "Go on, now," he said. He stood a blade's length from Jonas' leg.

Jonas drew his pistol. Moroyoqui whooped and beat the wings of his poncho over Copper's head. Copper sprang away. Jonas snatched his head around by one rein. Copper quivered and flopped his head from side to side and gathered momentum as he whirled. Jonas gave him his head so he would line out and he bucked straight for Moroyoqui. Jonas thrust his pistol at the Indian's face. Moroyoqui slapped it out of Jonas' hand with the machete and disarmed him as it fired. Copper reared and Jonas thought he would fall over backwards. Jonas gave up his deep seat and kicked his feet out of the stirrups so he could step clear if the horse fell. He gave Copper slack. Copper's head fell out of sight and he bucked through a gauntlet of laughing Yaquis who slapped him by with the flat sides of their machetes. He dove off a high bank into a wash. The Yaquis whooped and ran along the bank, watching Jonas ride. Jonas hooked Copper with his spurs and regained his seat. Copper ran into another bank and threw his head up. Jonas got his feet back in his stirrups. Moroyoqui came around on the bank and fired Jonas' pistol in Copper's face. Copper stampeded and lunged up another bank. Jonas turned his head downhill and hooked him in the shoulder. Copper swallowed his head again, bucked back into the wash and scattered Yaquis who had been chasing him. Jonas headed him up a steep bank to leave the wash. Copper scrambled at the top and flipped over backwards, kicking all four feet to the sky and landing on Jonas in the wash. Jonas thigh exploded against a rock underneath the horse.

Jonas held fast to one rein to keep Copper down. He knew the foot on the broken leg was wedged in the stirrup under the horse. Copper would drag him to death if he let him up.

The Yaquis circled Jonas and laughed. He saw his pistol hanging on Moroyoqui's forefinger. The Indian bent over him and laughed in his face through muddy teeth. Copper heaved to get up. Jonas kept him down and he rolled and wallowed on the broken thigh. A Yaqui lifted Jonas' hat off his head with the point of his machete.

"*Eres buen jinete para cuaco demonio*," said Moroyoqui. "You are a fitting rider for a demon horse."

"The rider of demons has become a broken-legged cockroach," said Jonas. He vomited into the bank and felt better. He grinned at Moroyoqui. "I guess that'll teach me not to chase Yaquis on a bronco."

"We were entertained," Moroyoqui said. He sliced the cinches of Jonas' saddle. Copper's tight barrel popped them open and the saddle was free. A Yaqui steadied Copper's head and he stood up without walking on Jonas. Moroyoqui rolled Jonas' thigh with the point of his blade to make sure it was broken. He unbuckled Jonas' cartridge belt and fastened it on his own waist. He reloaded the pistol. He vaulted to Copper's back. He hugged Copper with his heels and jerked his head high and held it there.

Copper trotted up the wash like an old dink, not even offering to buck. He was not the same horse Jonas admired with that Yaqui on him. He was ringing his tail and stargazing with his mouth open.

Moroyoqui came back and dangled Copper on his bit over Jonas' head. "Be thankful you are not holding your *menudos,* your gizzards, in your hand. Be thankful you are a mere Texan and not a Mexican."

The Yaquis left the wash. Jonas was alone. After a while his hat sailed over the bank and landed beside him. He examined the hand the Indian had slapped with the machete when he lost his pistol. He gave himself up to the wind and the pain.

Of all the damned poverty-stricken places to break a leg, Jonas thought. I picked the worst. My pelvis is probably broke, too. Well, I'll at least stay whole as long as I lie right here and keep my pieces all together. My pieces are still more or less arranged in the same place. If I move, I'll start scattering myself.

He picked up his hat and rolled the brim in his rough hands and gently brushed it. He remembered when it was so pretty he would not pick it up if his hands were dirty. A tear started in his eye. He swallowed and cleared his throat out loud to rid himself of its cause. He pulled his saddle to him and drank a swallow of water from his canteen. He rolled the canteen gently to measure the water.

"I don't have a full canteen, nor a full head of sense," Jonas said out loud. He laid the canteen down and picked up his hat again. He was reluctant to let go his hat. He loved that hat.

The hat lost its shape the time Maggie did a war dance on it in New York. It had been his drinking hat when it was new and good looking. That hat even made Jonas Ryan look good. It was so fine it made a man stand up straight so it would ride high where it belonged. When a man stepped out in that hat, the populace made way.

The hat had been a gift from Maggie for good behavior. It had lost its shape forever the time she jumped on it with both feet. Nothing keeps forever.

I'm lucky, Jonas thought. At least I'm out of the wind. A clear, whole and healthy tear dropped off his cheek and splashed on the back of his hand. He tried to wipe it away quickly, but it was stubbornly wet and big and dissipated slowly.

Bill was worrying about Jonas and the Breach brothers. He came in from guard at dawn and rolled out his bed for a few moments' rest. He made a cigarette, lay down on his blankets, covered himself with his tarp and smoked.

No crew in Arizona was big enough to hold the herd after three nights of windstorm. The whole outfit was sanded raw and about to turn tail and run for the shelter of some big, brushy canyon. Tom had relieved Bill on guard. Tom was grouchy and running out of reserves. Tom was the toughest cowboy Bill had ever known and the one with the finest character, but even Tom's good humor had been blown away by the storm.

Bill's bedroll contained a thin mattress, flannel sheets, two Hudson blankets and a tarp. Pascual was wrapped in a *serape* with his head on the ground, his feet naked to the storm in their *huaraches*. His legs were folded so the soles of the *huaraches* were to the wind.

"Wake up, Pascual," Bill said to himself, concentrating on the command without making a sound. "Wake up, Pascual," he said quietly. When Pascual stirred Bill said, "Are you resting?"

"Who can rest with a thousand worlds beating his carcass?" said Pascual. He yawned. "The whole world is faced back the way it came."

"They're going to run, Pascual," Bill said. "Sure as hell."

"They need room," Pascual said. "If we don't give it to them now, they'll take it by force."

Bill rolled and tied his bed, threw it into the hoodlum wagon and stomped to Cap's fire. Pascual tied his blanket to his saddle. Bill stepped away from the fire, located the remuda and motioned to Juan Charro to bring it in. He walked to Boots' bed and rolled him out.

Tom came riding in. He stood his horse away from the

fire. "We won't hold these cattle ten more minutes, Salty," he said. He was smiling and no longer gruff. The herd was out of his hands and in the grip of the storm. "We have to let 'em drift, or they're going to stick their horns in our ass and drive us home."

"Lordy, let's let 'em drift," said Bill, relieved. "Let's all get with our backs to the wind for a while. It'll do us a lot of good."

Boots was throwing his bed in the wagon.

"Have you got your pistol, Boots?" Bill asked.

"Got my rifle."

"Catch your horse. Catch Steeldust for me and stand by with Pascual. We're going to catch up to Jonas and the Breaches. I have a feeling they need a lot of help." He roused the crew and went to find Lindano.

Bill had been thinking about Lindano's hazing cattle off the herd every day, if that was what he was doing, then coming back and spending the night at the wagon. If he could come back, he must have partners receiving cattle on the edge of the herd. Bill probably had sent Jonas and the Breach brothers toward a lot of trouble. Lindano would not have gentle partners.

Lindano always slept away by himself. Bill found him under a bank in a wash where he could have peace from his cares. Off by himself, he could be sure he was not disturbed for some instant action regarding the herd in the night. He could also come and go without anyone knowing it. Bill stood on the bank above Lindano's head, watched him sleep and wondered why he was bothering to awaken him. He was not a child Bill had taken to raise. He would probably wake up feeling insulted, anyway. Bill did not need him. Maybe Juan Charro would also forget him and Lindano would wake up after the remuda and chuckwagon were gone, afoot, carrying his bed, and without his morning coffee. Bill turned away and went back to saddle his horse.

Bill, Pascual and Boots found Jake Breach on the Gila at

sundown. His campfire was behind a big cottonwood. The cattle he was holding were bedded in the lee of a sandbar. He gave no greeting when Bill and his partners rode up. His face was long. His look was sullen and antagonistic.

"Howdy," Bill said as he dismounted and began unloading blankets, canteens and provision. Jake sat and did nothing to help.

"How've you been making it, Jake?" Bill asked.

"We ain't making it. I've been with these cattle all day. Alex left early this morning to look for Jonas."

"When did you last see Jonas?"

"Yesterday morning, early."

"What happened to him?"

"I just know he hasn't showed up. Yesterday I had cattle when Alex and Jonas left me. Alex brought me twenty more last night. We had so much trouble holding the cattle we didn't have time to think of Jonas. Almost all the cattle slipped away from us last night."

"How far have you come since you last saw Jonas?"

"Who knows in this storm? You ride and you ride and you don't get anywhere, or even know where you are."

Pascual and Boots rode to meet Alex as he came off a hill with more cattle. Alex went to the fire and Boots and Pascual stayed with the cattle until they settled down.

"No Jonas?" asked Alex.

"He's probably laid out with his neck broke, or his throat cut," Jake said. "It's a cinch he didn't find a saloon. I'm ready for relief, myself. I'm damned ready to haul it back to the wagon."

"Listen, you're already in camp," said Bill. "This is home. The herd is drifting this way. Cap's wagons will be here tomorrow. We'll try to hold in the shelter of these trees until the storm quits."

"The wind is giving my brother trouble with his backbone," said Alex.

"I'm having trouble with my head," said Jake. "The dust

is clogging my sinuses; my head aches, I can't sleep, we ain't got nothing good to eat, I can't hear in this wind. Most of the time all I hear is the gravel peppering my hat. The cattle go everywhere but where I want them to go and I am nowhere, too. I'm not a cowboy, I'm a storekeeper. I don't want to be here."

The part of Jonas that still craved water was pinned to the bottom of the wash, but the part of him that did not need water was soaring in short flights away with Maggie. The Indian taking his hat had made Jonas remember he and Maggie had been at the Madison Square Garden Rodeo in New York when Maggie bought it for him.

Maggie always sat in the stand with the other wives and girl friends of the cowboys. Every time Jonas looked up at her, she smiled and waved at him. If he did not smile at her often enough during the show, she gave him a scolding later on. Jonas had been sleeping long hours with Maggie, dining regularly, and taking his booze moderately. He was sitting up straight on his broncs and making picture rides. He did not go on one toot the whole first two weeks he was in New York. His all around posture had been so rigid for so long he began to have sore places on his body. Another reason he was sore was that Maggie kept reminding him to be careful and not reinjure his old, crippled places. She was always asking him how he was feeling so she could be sure she was keeping him in condition to perform and that kept him thinking he was sore.

One evening, after two weeks of being good, Jonas ran out of control. He sang some dirty songs behind the chutes with the other cowboys. Paddy Ryan told jokes. Bob Askin found a bottle of whiskey nobody was using and they all cowboyed up beside it. The whiskey was so good they wanted more when it was gone. The whiskey reminded them life could be fun in town and they were in the best town for fun

in the world. They decided to roll out and find places that
served whiskey to the tune of music.

Maggie did not approve of Jonas running and playing.
After his last wild toot, she had gone out and bought herself
an elegant, nickle-plated, .32 calibre automatic pistol.
"Jonas," she told him when she caught him sobering up and
at a sad disadvantage. "If you ever get drunk and run off
and leave me again like you just did, I am not going to wait
at home for you like some sweet little thing. The minute you
turn up missing I'm coming after you and when I find you
I'm going to shoot the poop out of you."

Maggie was a big woman, twice Jonas' size. She was a good
woman, but she was mean when she was jealous. She meant
what she said. She was as jealous of Jonas' cowboy friends,
his top horse, his old dog, and his whiskey as she was of an
old floozie. The trouble was, Jonas was just like the scorpion.
He had to sting her now and then because the poison was in
him. The poison built up when he was riding good horses in
front of crowds of people. The minute the sun went down
in a town, the poison began smarting for release.

That evening when Jonas and his pals had ridden their
horses, they slipped out the door, loaded in a taxicab and
hit for the bars. Maggie was a talkative woman and did not
notice Jonas was gone until the last saddlebronc bucked out.
She quit talking when the other wives and girl friends stood
up to leave. She looked up and did not see Jonas. She stood
up and saw no pretty hat with Jonas smiling under it. She
rushed off for the taxi stand like a runaway ripsaw.

Tracking cowboys from speakeasy to speakeasy in New
York City was not difficult. Maggie could track a jack rabbit
over flat rock out in the country where she had no one to
give her directions. Every taxi driver who stopped his cab in
front of the Garden had some idea where cowboys went for
whiskey. Maggie began tracking Jonas.

The cowboys knew the perserverance and savagery of
their pursuer. They knew she would catch them if they

loitered in their drinking. They moved fast, drank deeply and changed springs often. They doubled on their tracks craftily. They pioneered trails to unlikely waterholes, places that had never heard of a cowpuncher and did not know one when they saw one.

Maggie tracked Jonas all night. She made false starts and turns. Some cabbies even tried to steer her off the trail because of their concern for their cowboy friends. They could see Maggie was one mad Texas Christian.

At dawn, Jonas and his partners fell out of a speak as it closed. Jonas looked up and Maggie's cab was sliding to a stop at the curb. Out piled Maggie, dressed in her best black dress and carrying a jeweled purse from which she pulled her shiny pistol.

"Hi, Maggie," said Jonas.

"Jonas, I'm gonna kill ya," said Maggie. "This is the last night of the world I spend chasing you, your whiskey bottle and your cheap friends. Now, you can stand and take your medicine like a man, you can run or you can fall on your knees and prepare your soul. I'm gonna count to three."

"Now, Maggie," said Jonas.

"One," said Maggie.

Jonas broke away so fast he ran out from under his new hat.

"Two," said Maggie, sighting her pistol.

Jonas cut toward the corner of the block.

"Three," said Maggie, and let a bullet fly. It creased the cheeks of his buttocks and rolled him in the gutter. He lay still, face down, and played dead. Maggie looked down. The new hat that had made Jonas look so handsome was lying at her feet. She jumped on it and did the Lindy Hop. Two of Jonas' partners loaded Maggie into her cab, ran her back to the hotel, helped her pack, and shipped her on the train back to Texas.

As soon as Maggie was out of sight, Jonas' other partners

picked him up, ministered to him, and carried him off to another speakeasy for a tonic.

Jonas spent two more weeks in the speakeasys while the world gave him up for dead. The Garden rodeo closed, his hangover caught up and he felt his duty to contact Maggie. He thought that over for a while and decided rather than go see her with a hangover, he should go to one more rodeo. He should make a little money so he could buy himself a drink and a new hat before he saw Maggie again. He figured if he contacted her too soon, he would only ruin any healthy remorse she might be suffering for shooting him. He would also surely reawaken her Texas Christian anger. His own happiness, not to mention his very life, would again be on the block for Maggie to do with as she saw fit.

After several more rodeos Jonas was just as broke so he headed for Texas, but at the last moment he ducked his head and passed through Maggie's country without reporting to her. His money ran out near the High Lonesome and he joined R.E. Bradford's herd.

Here he was, not a year after leaving New York, all busted up in a dust storm in Arizona, with no pards, no drink, no audience, no band music, and no Maggie to smile at. He did not regret one drink of whiskey he had swallowed, or one dance step he had tapped because he knew he had tapped his last dance. He wished he had Maggie's pistol now. He could put it to better use than she ever did. He could use it for an anesthesia.

"Oh, the things a cowboy'll run from and oh, the places he'll run to," Jonas said out loud. "I guess I've been lucky, though. I always got away, 'til now."

Bill, Pascual and Boots found the tracks of Copper, the cattle and the Indians heading north together toward the Yaqui encampments. After they followed the tracks awhile, Bill was sure Jonas was not riding Copper. He would not have followed the Indians with so much cooperation. Bill let

Pascual and Boots go on and he backtracked to see if he could find Jonas. He found the deep tracks Copper made when he bucked into the wash. He found Jonas lying with his back against the bank. His eyes were open and dry as burnt out coals.

"Aw, Jonas," Bill said softly. He dismounted with his canteen and dropped his reins so Steeldust would stand. He soaked his neckerchief and wiped Jonas' face and lips. He could find no pulse but when he bent over, he heard Jonas' breath on his ear.

"Honey, that is wet. That is nice," Jonas said distinctly. "Maggie, girl, what would I do without you?" The sound of him stopped then and his breath was gone.

Bill straightened. "Aw, Jonas," he said. He looked around at the dismal, empty wash that had been the end of Jonas' world. Nothing that stopped moving here could stay alive. "I haven't even got a shovel to dig you a hole." He could see how Copper had come off the bank and landed on Jonas. More cowboys died alone in a wash this way than ever died from bullets or whiskey. So why did everybody have such a fit when a cowboy had a good time?

Bill had noticed a place in a flat not far away where a fault had opened a wide crack in the ground. He cut ocotillo branches, tied them together and rigged a travois for Steeldust. He lashed Jonas on the travois, dragged him behind Steeldust to the fault where he laid the body in the crack, along with his saddle. He gathered rocks and covered Jonas. He stomped earth off the banks of the crack and smoothed it over the rocks with his hands. He staked a mesquite cross over Jonas' head and crowned it with the floppy hat. He took down the travois and laid the ocotillo over the grave. He stood by Steeldust and took off his hat.

"Lord, please give Jonas a gentle horse to ride, for a change," Bill said, and suddenly he could not keep from grinning. He mounted Steeldust and rode on, then stopped and took off his hat again. He wanted to say something nice, but he did not want to be a hypocrite. "Lord, if a gentle horse is what he wants," he added. He put his hat back on, trying to think of more to say since now was the time to say something right. Some preacher was sure to be found who knew the right thing to say. Someone was going to have to come back for Jonas' bones. Bill could not leave him in the wash. One rain shower would wash him down the country where they might never find him.

Bill turned back to see if Jonas' grave looked fitting. It did not even look like a grave. It only looked like a place where trash had gathered in a dust storm. He rode on to catch up to Pascual and Boots, thinking about Jonas' floppy hat bouncing and bucking in the wind on top of the cross and wondering how long it would stay.

Boots and Pascual stood their horses on a hill in sight of a Yaqui encampment. Two boys were herding ten HL and Breach brothers steers at the base of the hill. One of the boys was climbing a mesquite tree when he saw the horsemen. He dropped to the ground, ran and hid in the brush. His partner hid himself in a wash that ran by the encampment.

Pascual led Boots at a high trot off the hill toward the encampment. He did not look at the cattle as he rode by. Boots saw the cattle were full. They had watered. A horse nickered downwind, beyond the *jacal* shelter of the encampment. A fresh HL hide was staked to the ground by the *jacal*. Pascual and Boots stopped in the lee of the *jacal*, on its open side. Women and children stared at them from inside. Copper was tied to a tree in a swale below the *jacal*. He raised his head and nickered again. Boots's horse answered.

The women and children sat placidly in a row with no expression, as though not a bit surprised Pascual had come. A woman rose and stoked a fire with a mesquite branch.

"Where's your Mayo uncle, Genoveva?" asked Pascual in the Yaqui.

"Who knows?" said the woman. "He's not here."

"Where's the *Yori* who was riding the horse?"

"Moro brought the horse, that's all I know."

"Get Moro."

The woman motioned to the oldest of the girls, a tiny child with hair bleached orange by the sun and malnutrition. The hair looked as though it had been spun on her head by a spider. She ran to the wash.

"Have you water in your *noria*," asked Pascual.

"Yes."

"Will you give us permission to fill our *bules*?"

"Serve yourself, Matus."

Pascual handed his water gourd to Boots. Boots dismounted and went to a well that had been dug in front of the *jacal*. He reeled down a gourd bucket that was suspended by twisted rawhide on a windlass, brought up water and filled his canteen and Pascual's gourd.

Moroyoqui appeared with the child. He went into the *jacal* and dipped water from an *olla*, a fat, clay pot that sweated in the shade. He wet his lips, poured the water back into the *olla*, and floated the gourd dipper on top the water.

"Tell me, Matus," said Moroyoqui.

"Where's the *Yori* for that red horse?"

"In the wash where he fell off the horse, I am sure. He put himself there with a broken leg."

"Where?"

"South. An afternoon's ride on that horse you're riding."

"Where is Valenzuela, your brother?"

"Down in the wash with the pistol of the *Yori*."

"Skulking. You greet me with a skulk. You hide your eyes."

"We are not your friends."

"No, you are not, even though I spared you when I hanged La Carbonosa at Cedros."

"Spared me? You think the gringo's new rope would collar all your enemies?"

"You declare yourself my enemy, Moro?"

"I am not your friend."

"No, your skulking along on the edge of the herd has not been friendly."

"Our friend is the provender." Moroyoqui was standing so his eyes were shaded by the *jacal*. His frayed clothing fluttered on the edge of the wind. His long, thick hair stirred over his face. His great, horny feet were set like roots on the ground.

"I did not let you go free as a horse thief so you could leave my friend on the desert to die—so you could ride away on his horse and fill your belly with his beef."

"Should we have carried him here? This *jacal* is too poor for a *Yori*. We don't carry our own when they break their backs. Why should we carry a *Yori*? He put himself where we left him. He was not able to carry himself away. He has become part of the wash where he fell. It was his time. The cattle carried themselves here. The meat carries life for us. Would it not have been foolish for us to carry a dead *Yori* here? You and I have fallen in the fight against the Mexican. Have I been required to carry you, Matus? Have you ever carried me? If I was so required, I did not know it.

"Now we have meat. We did not separate the meat from your herd. Lindano gave it to us for our families. I have no concern for the *Yori* feelings about that. We did not take his cattle from him, or knock his cowboy off his horse."

"You're welcome to the meat. What is meat? Meat is for the hungry. You are not welcome to enjoy a friendship with Lindano. Do not touch another beef from this herd.

"Here on this desert of Arizona, the Yaqui has found refuge from Mexicans. This must continue to be his refuge. If you eat *Yori* beef to satisfy hunger, he won't care. If you sell *Yori* beef, steal horses, and leave good men to die on the desert, the Yaqui will be unwelcome here."

"Matus, I'm not running from the Mexicans as you are. I'm here because I'm tired of being poor. I wish to prosper.

I seek wealth. My brother, my cousins and I have no good intention of preserving refuge for the Yaqui."

"You admit you're here for banditry? God have mercy on you."

"*Egui turi,* yes, I very much admit it," growled Moroyoqui. He picked up an old French musket from behind a straw partition beside him and it was already loaded and cocked. Pascual had laid his rifle over his lap with the muzzle pointed away from Moroyoqui. He spun his horse while Moroyoqui brought the musket to his shoulder. Pascual's bullet struck Moroyoqui in the sternum. He collapsed over his sturdy feet and died with his forehead against the ground between his knees.

Boots felt a sting on his right hand. He looked down and watched a caprice of the wind snatching his little finger off his hand. He heard the report of a pistol, looked up and saw a man pointing a six-shooter over the bank of the wash. Pascual launched his horse straight at the Indian.

The Indian threw away the pistol as though it were an evil encumbrance and ran, yelling, "No, Pascual, no, Pascual, no, don't kill me."

Pascual rode him down, pressed the muzzle of his rifle between his shoulders with one hand and shot him on the run like a buffalo. He slid his horse to a stop as four other Yaquis flushed out of the wash and ran away in different directions. Pascual jumped his horse out of the wash and stood in his stirrups, waved his rifle, and whooped in derision for any living soul who might be listening.

Boots joined him, leading Copper. He had bound his kerchief over the stump of his finger and it sopped with blood. Pascual rode back to the front of the *jacal* where Moroyoqui's body lay. The women and children were not looking at Moroyoqui.

"Genoveva," said Pascual. "Your husband, Urbano, has run away across the flats and hidden from me again. This is the second time he has found it necessary to run from me.

If he ever comes near me again with his mischief you will keen alleluia on this desert with no man to take you home to the Rio Yaqui."

Boots and Pascual rode away to find Bill. The wind softened and spare moisture began touching them. As a good rain began to wet down the desert, they found Bill riding to meet them.

Bill gave Copper a dirty look and before he even said, "Hello," he told Boots to turn the horse loose. Boots slipped Jonas' bridle off and the horse shook his head and trotted away. "He'll never be worth a damn," Bill said. "He's got a notch in his tail. He killed Jonas."

As the men rode away from Copper, Boots looked back and saw the horse nuzzling under a chaparral for something to eat. Copper raised his head to meet Boots's gaze, nickered, thought a moment, and ran after the horsemen.

When Lindano woke he found he was all alone. The whole outfit had deserted him in the storm. As he rolled his blanket and saddled his mule, he noticed that the wind was settling down. He could no longer count on the weather and the trail to distract Bill and Tom—the crew was liable to run up on the tracks of the cattle he had turned over to Yaquis.

He decided he had done all the "cattle herding" he needed to do for the money Claire was paying him. He got on his mule and rode away in the direction of the nearest saloon.

CHAPTER 9

A horseman is fine in his posture among men.

THE herd browsed along with Red Rock in sight. The desert was still and fragrant from days of light rain.

Bill hoped he would see Mary that day. All she had to do was saddle a horse and ride out to meet the herd, but she was probably not even interested. The morning quiet in Bill and the morning spring in Steeldust's step were wearing out in the sun and Mary had not come.

Bill almost had forgotten how she looked. The rocks under his bedroll, the tired herd, the hard pace he kept, crowded out his picture of her. He could admit he wanted to see her now that she might be near. He was resolved to let her know how much he thought of her. She was grown and he wanted to make sure she knew he wanted her.

Bill rode to a hill to watch for Mary. The leaders of the herd were nearing the waterlot at headquarters. Bill saw Mary and R.E. riding toward him. He waved and they came on as he rode off the hill, happy.

Mary was smiling, but she remained quiet while she waited for R.E. to finish his business with Bill.

"Looks like the cattle are in fair shape and you made good time," said R.E., watching the herd. Bill was glad R.E. was intent on the herd because he wouldn't see Bill looking at Mary's face.

"We can account for the cattle, cowboys and horses that aren't here," Bill said.

"How many did you lose?" R.E. asked, drawing Bill's attention from Mary to the livestock.

"Give up thirty-six cattle for dead. We lost some at the cliff at Spring Mountain. Some died in the heat. The Yaquis took eleven head and one cowboy. We left about three hundred tired cattle behind."

"So, you're only thirty-six head short, but you didn't bring three hundred and thirty six head."

"We left some sore-footed cattle behind. We let tired cows and calves straggle. At least a hundred big steers quit the herd in the dust storm. The Breach brothers, Pascual and two others are bringing them."

"How long before they get here?"

"Three or four days."

"Good work, I guess."

"That's all we had to do, get them here. The storm hurt us."

"Which cowboy is missing?"

"Jonas went after eleven head some Yaquis were driving off and got himself killed on us."

"*No,* Bill."

"The colt he called Copper fell on him. He laid in a wash two or three days. I found him just the minute he died. I buried him, but he won't be hard to find. Pascual killed the main Yaqui. I guess nobody has to know that, do they?"

"Lord, no, but can't you crazy bastards find better ways to die?"

"Hell, that way was as good as any. It's what a man expects. Clean and no fuss, except for the one who's doing the dying."

"I'll notify the sheriff. We'll have to send somebody to guide him back. We can't just leave Jonas there, can we?"

"I guess he wouldn't mind."

"Does anybody know his next of kin?"

"We haven't looked through his gear, yet."

"Does anyone else know where you buried him? I need you here with me. I've got troubles."

"We can send Boots. He can see the doctor at the same time. The Yaquis shot his finger off."

"Okay. I wish all my troubles could be solved so easily."

"What other troubles have we got?"

"Claire will call in my note when he sees we're short three hundred and thirty six head. He and Kapp are waiting for an excuse to take the herd."

"We're only thirty six cattle short. We'll have the rest here soon enough."

"Claire's been hoping the storm would bring us in short."

"What kind of note does he hold?"

"He holds a lien on my herd."

"When's it due?"

"We have two weeks."

"Sell the big steers and pay him. Won't that cover it?"

"I was hoping it would, but thin as they are, the steers aren't merchantable. They need a hundred days on good feed to put on the flesh that would pay what I owe. Thin steers are worthless and feed is scarce. Only the cows and calves have any value. We couldn't find a steer buyer in the whole U.S.A."

"Where else did it rain?"

"It started raining on the Mexican Coast by Libertad a week before it rained here, and then it kept on raining down there. That might start the Indian wheat, down there."

"Let's take them to Libertad. We've done it before."

"Claire won't let us."

"How can he stop us? We'll drive that way and if we don't cross the line before the note is due, we'll give him the steers."

"That might be the way to go. I don't know what we'll do about the crew, though. Claire guaranteed their wages for the drive as far as Red Rock and I was counting on not having to pay that money. How can I ask the crew to go on without pay?"

"The crew will stay on. We'll take the same chances as the herd."

"Did Lindano give you any trouble?"

"He never let up. I'm almost sure he's the cause of Jonas' trouble."

"He's probably been slowing up the drive so you'd arrive just in time for his boss to foreclose."

"Where are Kapp and Claire?"

"They're here at headquarters, waiting."

"Today we cut Lindano and his bosses off this herd, by God."

"See if you can figure a way to keep my herd out of Claire's bank while I visit with Tom and Pascual."

R.E. rode away and left Mary and Bill looking at each other.

"I thought you were some old outlaw riding on that hill when I first saw you," Mary said, laughing.

"You get what you see. Can't improve today. I didn't see a barber, but we all bathed and washed our clothes at Kimbro's ranch last night."

"You look like you've been a'seein' the country, as Jonas would say. Poor Jonas. Daddy must have told that story about them seeing the country together a hundred times since it happened."

Bill looked away to see if he could find Boots to send him after the sheriff.

"When are you coming in town to see me?" asked Mary.

"Aw, you thought I looked funny when you saw me on the hill. How do you think I'd look to your college friends? Anyway, we're moving the herd on toward the line."

"Did you notice the horse I'm riding?"

"I sure did. Lizard don't look starved to death to me. What was wrong with him?"

"Doc Courtright came out to see him. His jaw wasn't

broken. Kapp's cowboys broke one of his back teeth when they threw him to cut him. Doc fixed the tooth."

"Kapp said the vet would cost more than the horse was worth. How much did he charge?"

"Doc only charged eight dollars."

Lizard looked up at Bill just as though he knew he was being talked about and he was certainly worth more than eight dollars. His muzzle looked slightly off center with his jaws.

"His face is out of line. He won't get any prizes for being good lookin' anymore."

"How's Steeldust doing? Haven't you been feeding him? He's lean as a snake. Kinda like his rider."

"Lean, mean and eatin' beef on the hoof. You're the one that looks good, Mary. You ought not to be out here where you can torture the crew with good looks."

"I'm happy. Today is the first time I've been on a horse since I left the ranch."

"You and Lizard would make any cowboy look at his hole card. You look beautiful together. I might just give him to you."

"You remember our deal, don't you? If I saved Lizard for you, you'd give me Steeldust."

"That's not the deal. I paid for Lizard. Your daddy ordered me not to make any horse deals with you."

"Well, let me take Steeldust home with me and give him a rest. He looks like he needs a little lovin'."

"All right, if you promise not to turn him against me. I might even give him to you someday if you ever grow up."

"What's grown up enough for you? I'll do anything to own that horse. Tell me what I have to do."

"Let's see how he behaves with you. You might not even like him anymore. He's making a cowhorse now. He's been a'workin' and he might see something he wants to turn and jump right out from under you."

"That kind of action suits me just fine."

"Get off old Lizard, then."

"Now?"

"Right now."

Bill put Mary's saddle on Steeldust and his own on Lizard. He and Mary rode to the herd. Bill did not want to leave the horse behind, but Steeldust was in the best of hands. Bill would be unfair to ask more of him now when he had a chance to rest and grow. He was still a youngster. Anyway, Mary must know he thought a lot of her if he let her keep his horse. He was not able to tell her any other way, not because he was afraid of her, but because he did not know the language of the *boo hoo kiss kiss* the girls and boys were known to enjoy. Everybody was better off, now. With Mary, Steeldust would think he had died and gone to heaven.

Bill watched Steeldust carry her away toward the house. Steeldust already seemed to be thriving under her voice and hands, which just went to show a top horse often made his own best deals.

The herd was counted into the waterlot and was three hundred and forty cattle short. Bill gave the crew instructions to join him while the herd was watering. The men gathered at the wagon and Cap poured coffee. R.E. rode up on Bob Kane.

"Before you men make plans about going to town, I've got to tell you we're moving the herd on down the Altar Valley into Mexico," R.E. said. "Nobody who stays with the herd will be paid his wages in full today. I hope you'll all stay, but if you need all your money, we'll have to let you go."

Juan Charro stepped forward. He was always one who loved to argue for his rights and make sure he walked away with every penny he could grab.

"I, for one, wish to be paid all my wages," said Juan Charro.

R.E. reached inside his saddlebags. "I have your money," said he. "I have the cash to pay every one of you in full.

Understand me, if I pay all your wages, you have to roll your bed."

Juan Charro bowed his head. "I wish to continue working, but I need to see your money."

R.E. unlaced his saddlebags, brought them down off his horse and spread the money on the ground in front of the crew.

"How do we know we'll be paid when we come back with the cattle?" asked Juan Charro.

"You don't know," Bill said. "If you're worried about that, take your money. If you wait, I'll buy all the drinks the first night we're back here with the herd."

"You know I don't drink. I don't need drink. I need pay."

"Take your pay and roll your bed," R.E. repeated.

"I'd like a third of my wages, at least, so I can clothe myself," said Juan Charro. "My clothes are worn out. I am a working man. I'm a horse wrangler and a trader. I'm a business man who concerns himself with money. I am not easily fooled in money matters." He took his money from R.E. and sat against the trunk of a tree to count it, separating the different bills.

"You'll be taking the herd all the way to the Mexican Coast," R.E. said to the crew. "You won't start back toward the High Lonesome until April. I won't blame you if you don't want to go. I thank you for your work on the drive so far."

Tony stepped up. "I'm staying with the herd. I always wanted to go to the Mexican Sea," he said.

"Fine. Does anybody want to take his money and leave now?" asked R.E.

"I think we'll all stay until we take the herd back to the High Lonesome," said Tony. "That's what we hired on to do."

"All right, I'm paying each of you fifteen dollars. You'll have a chance to go to town before we're out of range of the dry goods and the saloons."

The herd was moving the next day when Kapp's roadster caught up. The car headed toward Bill, carrying the blank faces of Kapp, Claire and Lindano. Bill was riding Lizard and keeping his attention on the herd. The roadster crept up behind Lizard and honked. Tired cattle scattered away and Lizard hunched, goosed himself with his own tail and scampered away from the roadster. The cattle settled down and continued on their way. Bill grinned at the stern faces in the machine. Kapp stopped the car and Lindano stepped down. Kapp sat up and gazed away into the distance as though the seat of the roadster was his throne and he could watch his domain better through a windshield. Claire was wearing his three-piece suit, saving action and gesture as if he kept a strict accounting of the motion expended throughout the day. Bill moved Lizard up close to the roadster so he could stand slightly behind Claire and over his head. Lizard did not like standing by the machine and Claire did not like having to look back at Bill.

"Get off and let's go," said Kapp, looking straight ahead through the windshield. "Give your horse to Lindano."

Claire looked away at the herd with his nose in the air. He did not mind stealing the herd R.E. had spent a lifetime building, but he did not want to get any of it on his suit. Lizard fidgeted too close to him and made him uncomfortable, but he would not look back. Tony was riding toward the car.

"Well, well, R.E.'s partners," Bill said. "I thought you fellers would have left the country on some *big* deal, by now. You didn't stay to clean up on this little herd, did you?"

Kapp chuckled indulgently. "Get in," he said.

"In a hurry, are you?" Bill asked. He was watching Claire squirm in his seat.

"For hell's sake, let's move," said Claire.

"Cattle barons," Bill said. "Drove all the way out here to find us and can't stand the cattle, men and horses part of it." He dismounted and handed Lizard's reins to Tony. If

Tony had learned anything from Bill, he would know not to let Lindano ride Lizard. Bill climbed into the back of the roadster and Kapp drove away.

Kapp and Claire watched Bill out of the corners of their eyes and he grinned at them all the way to R.E.'s house at Red Rock. They did not say a word to each other: they had enough to do keeping an eye on Bill in case he tried to do them mischief.

Bill dismounted from the roadster and followed them to the front door of R.E.'s house. He took off his hat and spurs and tried to smooth down his hair before R.E. met them at the door. Mary brought coffee on a tray and led them across a shiny, hardwood floor toward the office. No one said a word. Mary's heels chipped delicately at the hard floor and the boot tops of the men slapped against their legs as they walked through the cool, silent house.

Kapp sat himself in R.E.'s chair behind a desk in the den and chuckled again. He picked a cup of coffee off the tray as soon as Mary poured it and paid her no mind. Claire closed the drapes on all the windows, just as though he was in his own home. He sat in a straight chair against the wall beside the desk.

"Just make yourselves at home and have coffee," said R.E.

Claire dropped his hat on the floor beside the chair. Kapp shoved his hat to the back of his head and folded his arms. He was enjoying himself. He was bringing about a reckoning he had been waiting for. Time to figure the dollars. Time to show who was right about business. Bill was thinking, these men always figured they were in the right when they were making decisions in their offices, their roadsters, their booths in their bars. If the man on the horse came up short of cattle, he paid them. Everybody paid them on days like this.

Bill sank into an easy chair and watched Claire open a brief case and take out an accounting sheet. The man studied the numbers on the sheet. He leaned the back of the chair against the wall and the tips of his toes just touched the floor.

"Bill, we know you and R.E. are trying to pull something on us," said Kapp. "Just tell us what it is and we'll try to work it out."

"You bet we are," Bill said.

"What?"

"We're trying to keep the herd on feed and water. We like to see cattle do good."

"Uh, huh," said Kapp, in a good humor. He watched Claire work his pencil on the numbers.

"How many big steers in this herd now?" asked Claire, without looking up.

"About four hundred," said R.E.

"Just a minute, I want Shane to answer," Claire said.

"The answer's the same no matter who gives it to you," Bill said. "We have about four hundred HL steers and a hundred and fifty neighbor steers, enough to settle R.E.'s account. You must have agreed on the value of the steers when you loaned R.E. money on the herd."

Claire looked down his nose at Bill. He was not used to being given answers he did not like. Kapp chuckled and drooled around his cigar. His mouth was small and shaped like a baby bird's with a tiny, fleshy beak on the upper lip that pecked softly and moistly at the cigar. His spirit was in Claire's bank vault and his eyes had the color and imperviousness of its steel door. He had to be tough to drool like that. Bill's spit was drying up.

"You haven't been authorized to move these cattle beyond Red Rock," Kapp said. "You're short cattle. You say they'll catch up, yet you move on. What happened to the big steers you started with?"

"Nothing we can't account for. We lost thirty-six cattle in all. That includes bulls, cows, calves, oxen, all kinds, not just big steers. Your man, Lindano, tried to waste cattle every chance he got. Ask him why he hurried cattle in the heat.

Ask him how the Yaquis took hold of eleven head. We cut the brands out of the hides of all the cattle that died on the trail. We have the patches at the wagon. We lack only the brands from eleven head the Yaquis ate. Pascual and Boots and poor old Jonas Ryan's carcass are witnesses to the Yaquis' taking those cattle and your man Lindano's part in it."

"I know for a fact that a big, black steer is missing, because I wrote down his markings when the herd left the High Lonesome," said Kapp. "What happened to him? Did he weaken and die, too?"

"Are you inquiring after a big, good looking, healthy, shiny, black steer that had real pretty horns that stood way out from his head with black tips on them?"

"Yes, one of the biggest steers, a young steer."

"We ate him."

"Ate him?" Kapp chuckled. "Ate him?"

"Hell, yes. We butchered him on the trail. We ate the one that was in the best flesh. He was a good choice, too. Tender as hell."

"Well, you ate the steer that was worth the most money."

"Be careful, you're admitting they're worth money," R.E. said.

"Yes, we'll probably eat another one just like him," said Bill. "We had to kill the black steer before we made jerky of the cattle killed in a fall from a cliff when the herd ran off Springs Mountain. On the trail you don't wait for cattle to die before you decide you can eat beef."

"I can't understand that," said Claire.

"No, I guess not. Salamanders don't eat beef," said Bill.

"Now, I guess, you think you're taking the herd to Mexico," said Kapp. "Is that where you think you're headed?"

"That's where we're headed."

"We want the note paid before the cattle are lost to us in Mexico. You can understand that, can't you?"

"They won't be lost in Mexico. It rained down there. This

is not the first time we've taken the herd to Mexico. We'll be among friends. We'll have good feed."

"You understand we hold a lien on this herd? We have money in it. We're within our rights to hold the cattle here."

"Bring somebody tough when you get set to hold us. After forty-five days on the trail eating sand with our biscuits, you two white mice won't do it."

"What are you willing to do about paying the note, R.E.?" asked Claire.

R.E. had been listening to his chair creak as the banker put it under stress by leaning its back against the wall. "When you bought into my herd you took on the luck of the draw the same as me," R.E. said. "I understood you were investing so you could help me. I gave you an interest in the fortunes of my cattle for your money. You took a lien for protection in the event something chaotic happened between the High Lonesome and Red Rock. Now you want to call in my note before we find a haven or a sale for the cattle. As far as I'm concerned, the herd arrived in good shape for your inspection and my responsibility is to go on and see it keeps producing. You bought a third of that program. However, I can see you never intended to act as my partner. You only wanted my herd."

"Your former herd has been depleted," said Claire. "This is not the same herd I invested in. You're missing a great many cattle and you intend to take it away to a catastrophic situation in Mexico. I don't know a more scarified situation for my money. How will you ever satisfy my lien?"

"I stopped worrying about that. You're my partner. The herd is headed for a place where it will grow in value, on good feed. We won't worry about them so much and we'll have time to look for a buyer. Try to stop us and we fight. We'll fist fight, gun fight, do anything to get past your lien to Mexico."

"We'll call the law. There'll certainly be no fight," said Claire.

"We'll fight here in this room and leave the law out of it," Bill said.

"Listen, from our point of view, you're only trying to avoid paying what you owe," Claire said, still positive he was right and therefore was bound to have his way.

"Come up with the payroll you promised," R.E. said. "Find us some feed so we can keep the cattle here. Keep our credit alive. Think of the trouble you'll have if you take over the herd."

"I'm holding out on the payroll. I'll not pay your crew to move my cattle out of the country."

"You're forfeiting your interest in the cattle, then. You were made a partner for your money."

"What's your position, Shane?" asked Claire. "You ought to talk to the crew. I don't think the men want to go to jail over this sorry herd."

"Hell, we cowboy for R.E. Bradford. You think we don't take risks? We cowboy up. We've been stepping over that snake Lindano on our way to our bedrolls for six weeks. Taking the herd past you won't bother us."

"What are you making for your part in this, Shane?" asked Kapp.

"Wages, when R.E. has money. That's the only kind of money I know. I work for a cowman. I don't make money conniving over his paper."

Kapp took the cigar out of his mouth and struck a match to it. "You're not making anything at all, not even wages, Shane. We own the cattle and your wages. Your boss took our money and spent it. Now he's in trouble with his crew, his bank, and the law. You must figure on going to jail with your boss, you're so true blue. Walk away from his deal and we'll pay all the wages owed you and the crew. You can stay with the herd, expect a bonus when it's sold and you won't have to take chances in Mexico."

"There you are, Bill," said R.E. "The chance of a lifetime. All I ever did was give you a horse."

"We fight," Bill said. "I don't think I want to wait much longer for it. I'll get all my fightin' out of the way right here when I stand out of this chair."

Kapp pecked and savored his cigar. "You'll suffer a loss, cowboy," he said. "Stand up out of that chair for anything but your hat and your life is over. I'll put the law on your tail."

"If you do, it will be the first time you tried to be on the same side as the law."

"If you know that, you know how easy it would be to hire a deer hunter to put you down," Claire said.

Bill crossed the room and kicked Claire's chair out from under him. Claire went down with his head crammed against the wall. Kapp raised up as Bill poised his boot heel over Claire's head.

"I'll just settle this right now by stomping your eyes shut," said Bill.

"If you're going to hurt my banker, do a good job," Kapp said. "If I go to the poor house, I want to see them hang you."

Claire bellowed, "Kapp, you son of a bitch, get him off."

"Here, Bill," R.E. said quietly. "Not in the house. Take him outside to stomp him."

"Calm down," said Kapp. "That's my *credit* down there under your heel."

"All right, Kapp, let's settle this while your partner is in a position to deal," Bill said.

"Okay, don't hurt him and we'll deal," Kapp said. He laid his cigar on the desk and it rolled off, forgotten.

"We'll cut you three hundred of the big end of the steers to buy you out," R.E. said. "That's all we'll do."

"That's fine. That's okay," said Claire, showing the palms of his hands.

"Let him up now," said Kapp.

Bill stepped back and Claire untangled his legs from the chair and stood up. "I didn't want this kind of trouble,"

Claire said. His hair stood up on the back of his head from the scraping the wall had given it on his way to the floor.

"No more argument," R.E. said. "Let's see the lien."

Kapp dug the lien out of Claire's brief case and spread it on the desk in front of Bill. "Now, what do you want changed about this?" he asked.

"Hand it to me, Bill," R.E. said.

Bill handed it over and R.E. tore it up. "You backed out on our agreement when you sent Lindano to devil the drive," R.E. said. "We're cutting out your cattle for you, giving you a bill of sale, and putting an end to the fuss."

Bill, R.E. and the ex-partners headed through the house toward the front door. Mary passed Bill, stepped in front of Claire and blocked his way. Bill knew he was probably in for a scolding from Mary for kicking a chair out from under the banker—not the kind of behavior that would heighten Mary's social season.

Claire set his jaw and tried to step around the girl, but Mary stamped on his toe and nailed him in place.

"Claire, I just want you to know, you aren't welcome here, anymore," Mary said. "Don't ever come here with your scummy business deals again."

"Now, Mary, this is man's business between your father and me and his hired help," Claire said. "Don't be smarting off at me, or butting in."

"A man's business? You're trying to give a man the business, you mean."

"Now, Mary," said R.E.

"No, Daddy, this man is jealous of everything we own. I want him to know we won't dance with him or his kid just because he's a banker. And another thing, I want him to keep that Lindano away from us. I'll shoot him with your gun, that's what I'll do."

Kapp lit himself a new cigar, dropped the wrapping on the floor, looked out the door and chuckled.

"Pete Kapp, you greedy slob, you were never welcome

here," said Mary. "Do you know I wipe your chairs with disinfectant after you leave? Anyone who would treat a horse the way you did Lizard must have some dread disease."

Kapp chuckled and turned to her. "Girl, you'd better go to your Mama. Don't pick fights with me. I make little girls like you suck eggs and breathe through their ears."

Bill shoved Kapp out the door. Kapp bounced on the veranda on his toes and grinned. He took off his shirt and draped it carefully over the porch rail.

"Now, you and me are going to fight, Shane," Kapp said. He spit out the cigar. "Just drop the spurs."

Bill looked down and saw he was still holding his spurs. He handed them to R.E.

"Get him, Bill," said Mary.

Surprised at Mary, Bill walked straight into Kapp's right fist. He shook his head as Kapp danced back; then he stepped in, hit Kapp on his soft little beak and knocked him off the veranda. He gave him time to stand up and knocked him down again.

"Now, you're fixing it for yourself, idiot," shouted Claire. "You'll answer formal charges for this."

Kapp was spitting blood.

"Hell, Pete, I thought you wanted to fight," Bill said. "Did you think you could whip me by baring your physique?"

"Shall I go to my Mama, now?" asked Mary sweetly.

Claire stepped around Kapp's carcass and walked out the front gate toward the roadster. Bill took hold of Kapp's arm and helped him up. Kapp wiped his mouth and leered at Mary.

"That's going to be a great little piece for somebody soon," Kapp said.

Bill turned to see if Mary had understood what he meant and Kapp clubbed him behind the ear. Kapp hit him in the eye and Bill knocked him down again. Kapp began crawling in circles on his hands and knees. Bill walked around in front of him to put the cowboy stomp to him, then decided against it because Mary was watching.

"Stop this, now," said R.E. "Step away from him, Bill. Let him up. Go in the house and wash your face."

Bill went to R.E.'s bathroom and looked at himself in the mirror. Kapp's ring had cut him on the bridge of his nose next to the eye and had cut a hole in his cheek. The scars would not be dashing. He washed his face and Mary came in with a compress to stop the bleeding. He sat on the toilet seat and when she stood close to him he could feel the warmth of her breath.

"Put your head back, Bill. Look at you. I thought you could fight better than that. We're a hell of a team, all right. You're good at being walloped, I'm good at cheering it on— and Daddy holds the spurs well. We could get a match any day with that kind of talent."

"I could have been fighting instead of worrying about you, that's for damned sure," Bill said.

Mary pressed her starched dress against him. The touch and sound of her breath caressed him as she daubed at his cuts with cotton and Mercurochrome. She put aside the medicine, wrapped her arms around his neck and kissed him. Her face stretched the cut on his cheek and her forehead bumped his sore eye. She cocked her head to one side to look at him.

"More," said Bill. "Do more of that."

"Are you sure I'm grown enough for you, mister? Don't you think it's time we gave each other some lovin'?" asked Mary.

"Yes, Mary."

"How do you feel about all this? Tell me."

"Do all that to me some more."

"I'll close your other eye if you don't tell me how you feel about me."

"Dammit, I usually look way off when I feel love. I'm not

used to talking this close to you. I'm still watching you grow."

"You can't watch me grow. I grow when you aren't looking."

"I've been in an awful state about that, Mary." Bill said and kissed her.

"Don't keep so far away from me, anymore. I know you, so don't be making big circles around me. Don't mess around those girls when you go off down to Mexico, either."

"I guess I better not."

"I guar-an-dam-tee you better not," said Mary. She stepped back to give him room. He felt like his own skin was taking itself away.

R.E. came looking for Bill, loaded him in his car and drove to the herd. Tom rode up and R.E. told him to pen the herd at a neighboring ranch.

"You better get your horse, Salty Bill," Tom said, giving Bill an accusing look. "Lindano's riding him to death."

Bill saw Lindano riding Lizard away from Kapp's roadster. Lizard was shining with sweat. His head had a stubborn, headlong tilt to it. He was slinging froth off his bit and his neck was arched under Lindano's heavy hand. Bill jumped down from the car and ran to head him off. He stopped in front of Lizard.

"Get off the horse," Bill said.

Lindano slumped in his seat and grinned at Bill. "You're the one on the ground now. How does it feel to be afoot and on your way to jail?"

Bill took hold of Lizard's rein and reached to unbuckle the throat latch on the bridle. "Step off or I'll snatch his bridle. He's so hot he won't pull up until he's home on the High Lonesome."

Lindano spurred Lizard, knocked Bill down, and loped away, laughing. Bill picked himself off a bed of prickly pear and cholla cactus. The needles were pinning his brush jacket to his hide. He peeled off the jacket and began picking out the spines. He took off his shirt and picked at the hard, fine, prickly spines as he walked after Lindano. Tom rode to meet him.

"Where's your horse, Salty Bill?" asked Tom. He dismounted and picked cholla out of Bill's back while Bill examined his shirt and jacket and hands for stickers.

"How come he's on Lizard?" asked Bill.

"He rode him to the herd after you left in the car."

"Hell, I handed him to Tony. What did Tony say?"

"Didn't say a thing. He laughed when Lizard jumped out from under Lindano, though."

"Did Lizard buck him off?"

"Lizard turned back a cow and stood Lindano on his head. I saw it. Drove his hat down over his ears, as usual. Then, old, dumb Lizard just stood there surveying his damages."

"Too bad Lizard was ground hitched. He could have run off and been rid of the son of a bitch."

"Too bad, because Lindano kicked him plenty in the belly before he mounted, and he's been a'spurrin' and a'jerkin' him ever since."

Bill put on his shirt and jacket. Tom was riding cranky Jon. He mounted, slipped a foot out of the stirrup and said, "Get on behind me, Bill."

Bill stepped up and mounted behind the cantle. Jon took one look at his new burden, growled once and bucked Bill off sky high before he could even find a hand hold. Down into the cholla Bill landed again.

"Oops," said Tom. "That might have been a mistake. Damn, Salty Bill, there must be other places you could come to ground. The cholla ain't here to break your fall. It's only for the desert's adornment, they tell me."

"Well, it's a'dornin' me today," Bill said. He rolled over and unstuck himself from his jacket and shirt. Tom dismounted and helped clean him up again.

Bill dressed again. Tom mounted Jon, looked at Bill,

kicked his foot out of the stirrup and said, "Get on. He'll carry double."

"Yeah, double tough," said Bill. He walked wide of the gaze of the horse's evil eye and headed for the herd. He was catching up as the drags went through the gate of a neighbor's waterlot. R.E. and Lindano, Kapp and Claire were standing at the gate.

"Bill Shane," shouted Lindano. He stepped out in front of his bosses and glared at Bill.

Bill checked himself before he stretched his legs to hurry. He fixed on Lindano, took his time, and every step made him feel better as he advanced toward the man. The bigshots had undoubtedly primed Lindano to break Bill's nose and he had to face Bill and go to battle. But Bill knew Lindano would try to get around behind any man he fought, even here in the open.

"Don't worry, Lindano, I'm headed straight for you," said Bill when he was close enough so Lindano could hear him speak softly.

"I don't want you without your horse. I want you on your horse," Lindano shouted, before Bill was in range to hit him.

Bill felt a great and final satisfaction. The time had come to put the run on Claire's whole outfit. Lindano's calling Bill's name out loud put the match to Bill's fuse. Bill walked away and found Lizard. He untied him from a post in the sun where Lindano had left him to wet down the sand with his sweat. He knelt and took off his spurs, buckled them together and held them in his hand.

"Don't fret, anymore, Lizard," said Bill. "Today the ape draws his pay." He rode back to the gate.

"Here," said Lindano, gritting his teeth and grabbing Lizard's reins close to the bit. "Stand that horse right here and help count the cattle for my employers."

Just to be sure nothing else went wrong, Bill raised his spurs over Lindano's head, swung them by their straps and let them fall on the crown of his hat. The blow drove

Lindano's knees into the ground. Bill stepped off Lizard and dropped the spurs on Lindano's head again. Lindano fell on his face with his hat in his eyes. Bill kicked off the hat, lifted him to his knees by his hair and harelipped him from his nostril to his lower lip with the spurs. He left him for dead and remounted Lizard.

"Pick up your fighter, Claire," Bill said. "Clear the gate."

"You've killed the man," said Claire.

"No, I just marked him for life. I hope, if you bigshots ever have ideas of taking over this herd again, you send that son of a bitch so I can notch his other side."

Bill stood Lizard away from the gate. "Now, take your fighter out of the gate. We're about to count your cattle out to you."

Tom rode in to cut the big steers out of the waterlot. The first four were headed out the gate together before Kapp and Claire could help Lindano to his feet. The steers snorted and shied and jumped and kicked their tails high over Lindano's head as they rushed by. Kapp and Claire dropped him and ran. Tom rode back for more cattle. Kapp and Claire dragged Lindano to the shade of a mesquite.

Bill saw Tony ride around the outside of the waterlot with R.E., taking position to hold the steers. Bill was as angry at Tony as he was at the rest of Claire's outfit. Tony would be the next one he cut off the herd.

Tom finished cutting out the three hundred steers for Claire. The crew let the steers stream slowly past R.E., Kapp and Claire so they could be counted and inspected once more. The number of cattle and their price was agreed upon. R.E. gave them a bill of sale and was finally rid of his partners. They lifted Lindano into the roadster and left. Bill rode around Claire's herd toward Tony. Tony headed back to help the HL crew with R.E.'s herd.

"Where you headed now?" asked Tom.

"I'm running off the other banker," Bill said.

"The kid?"

"The Baby Fat."

"Better think about it."

"If he's going to be a banker, he might as well leave the company of cowboys now before we spoil him."

"Wait a minute. Talk to me."

"I'll be back in a minute."

Bill rode on. Tony saw him coming and moved off in a different direction. Bill rode up behind him.

"Claire," Bill growled.

"What."

"Pull up, or I'll run you down."

Tony stopped his mule. Bill rode up beside him. "You missed your ride. You should have caught the roadster with your own kind."

"Are you firing me?"

"I need the horses you're riding and I don't want your damned mules in our remuda."

"R.E. said I could keep the job as long as I talked it over with you. I'd like to stay, Bill."

"How do you figure on becoming a proper salamander if you stay with us?"

"That's my business."

"Sometimes R.E. sure is dumb. If I let you stay I'd be just as dumb."

"No matter which of us is dumb, I'd still like to stay."

"Listen, what more could you want from us? You haven't made a friend on the crew."

"I'm not asking for friendship, just work."

"Suit yourself," Bill rode away.

R.E. cut out Lindano's mules and threw them in with the steers. He took part of the crew and drove Claire's stock to his feedlot.

Tom rode up beside Bill. "I see you didn't run the boy off," he said.

"R.E. said he could stay."

"Good. He wants to make a hand."

"He wants to stay so he can cause contention."

"I don't think so. He's changed a lot."

"He's from the wrong stock, Tom. He is a son of a banker who is a son of a bitch."

"Well, don't say that about the kid. He's been good to you."

"How do you figure?"

"Didn't anyone tell you what he did this morning?"

"No."

"Remember I told you Lizard piled Lindano's ornaments in the dirt this morning?"

"Yeah."

"Tony wouldn't let Lindano ride Lizard after you left in the car, so Lindano beat Lizard with the quirt so he would break away from Tony. Tony jumped off his mule and took the quirt away from him, but Tony's mule ran off. Lindano mounted Lizard and left Tony afoot. That's why Lindano was on the horse when you showed up."

"What kept *you* from taking Lizard away from Lindano?"

"Hell, I figured you'd take care of it when you came back. The kid cowboyed up for you, though. Don't be hard on him, he's trying."

Bill rode after the herd awhile and thought about Tony and watched him. Lindano's quirt was hanging on Tony's saddlehorn. He rode over to him.

"I guess I was wrong, Tony," Bill said. "I appreciate you taking the quirt away from Lindano."

"I knew you would think I handed the horse over to him."

"I know what happened now. I carry no grudges. I didn't mean it when I said you had no friends in the crew. We all feel good about the way you've been making a hand."

Bill offered his hand and Tony shook it. Then Tony looked off to the northeast, behind Bill. Bill turned and saw Boots and the sheriff and two deputies coming with a pack horse. The horse was loaded with Jonas' body, wrapped in a new tarp.

If you have enjoyed this book and would like to receive details of other Walker Western titles, please write to:

Western Editor
Walker and Company
720 Fifth Avenue
New York, NY 10019

BRO

7.29

Brown, J. P. S.

Steeldust

DATE			

© THE BAKER & TAYLOR CO.